# Tritely Challenged

Volume 1

Copyright © 2018 Christopher Fielden. All rights reserved.

The copyright of each story published in this anthology remains with the author.

Cover copyright © 2018 David Fielden. All rights reserved.

Chris's Colossal Cliché Count Writing Challenge was launched in conjunction with the inaugural Flash Fiction Festival.

First published April 2018.

The rights of the writers of the short stories published in this anthology to be identified as the authors of their work has been asserted in accordance with the Copyright, Designs and Patents Act 1988.

All rights reserved. No part of this publication may be reproduced, stored in a retrieval system, or transmitted in any form by any means, electronic, mechanical, photocopying, recording or otherwise, without the prior permission of the publishers.

You can learn more about Chris's Colossal Cliché Count Writing Challenge and many other writing challenges at:

www.christopherfielden.com

All characters in this publication are fictitious and any resemblance to real persons, living or dead, is purely coincidental.

ISBN: 1986635619
ISBN-13: 978-1986635615

## DEDICATION

In memory of Laura Simmons.

# TRITELY CHALLENGED

*Jude Higgins (2nd from left) and Chris Fielden (bottom middle) with a gaggle of writers at the launch of* Flash Fiction Festival One, *an anthology containing stories written by festival attendees, speakers and organisers*

# INTRODUCTION 1

## by Jude Higgins

The inaugural flash fiction festival, the only literary festival in the UK – and possibly the world – dedicated to short-short fiction took place in Bath in June 2017. I was delighted when Christopher Fielden offered to host a workshop at the festival. It made sense to focus on one of his fun fiction challenges, which would give participants an opportunity to have their very short fictions published in a charity anthology. We came up with the idea of cliché-packed fictions.

Clichés sneak into fiction often without being spotted – as quick as lightning, in the blink of an eye, taking their place as bold as brass. They lurk in the middle of sentences, but can also frame your fiction when they involve whole storylines as well as metaphors – an exaggerated example would be men with manly chests and women with heaving bosoms meeting in the supermarket, exchanging harsh words over the last Christmas pudding, then hating each other. Such characters always come together again, find each other's redeeming features, fall in love and live happily ever after.

Many versions of this classic tale exist in fairy stories, in films and all sorts of literary contexts. Shakespeare has used versions of such plots and has also given us well-used phrases like 'lily-livered', 'all that glitters is not gold', 'wild-goose chase', 'green-eyed monster' and 'pure as the driven snow' among many others. It's a lot of fun deliberately including these phrases, and all the many other clichés embedded in our consciousness, in a piece of writing.

Many people at the festival told me they enjoyed letting go and breaking the rules when they wrote a story packed with clichés. Writing something deliberately 'bad' can create all sorts of new ideas. It's definitely to be recommended. We're pleased that the festival participants who gave the challenge a go feature in the book.

When the festival team learned that proceeds from the book were going to Book Aid International, we decided to complement funds raised from the book and donated the money raised from our festival raffle to the same charity. We were able to send a cheque for over £300.

The next flash fiction festival will take place on the weekend of 20th-22nd July 2018, this year in Bristol. Christopher's not available, so we won't have a cliché challenge, or one of his other challenges, at the festival, but writers can come along, attend workshops given by international presenters on all sorts of aspects of flash fiction and still create a first draft that breaks the writing rules. Not worrying about first drafts is always a good way to keep the energy going in writing. It makes the editing process more fun. And in the end it helps you write well.

Jude Higgins
Flash Fiction Festivals, UK, Director
www.flashfictionfestival.com

# INTRODUCTION 2

## by Chris Fielden

Welcome to the first cliché challenge anthology.

Chris's Colossal Cliché Count Writing Challenge was launched in June 2017 in conjunction with the UK's first ever festival dedicated to flash fiction, which took place in Bath.

Many of the stories in this book were written at the festival, by attendees. After the festival, I opened the challenge up to general submissions on my website. We received our 100th submission at the beginning of February 2018.

At the time of writing, we've already received some fabulous stories for the second anthology.

As sure as eggs are eggs (see what I did there?), many writers overuse clichés. To stand out from the crowd (see what I did there again? OK, I'll stop it now...), a writer needs to develop an original voice that the reader can identify and engage with. Clichés detract from this and often lead to rejection from magazine editors and competition judges.

The cliché challenge was launched to highlight this common mistake, give writers the experience of being published, support an amazing charity and to have fun with words.

When I undertake critiques, I often find myself advising other writers to avoid clichés. I *always* advise writers not to use clichés as a story title, unless there's an incredibly good reason to do so (I have yet to encounter an incredibly good reason).

This challenge does the polar opposite. It invites writers to stuff as many clichés into a story as humanly

possible. This can include:
- hackneyed phraseology;
  - 'in the blink of an eye'
- clichéd characters;
  - the drunk cop who wants to solve the case he's been working on for 20 years before he retires
- clichéd storylines;
  - the woman who is secretly using a dating website and goes on a romantic encounter only to discover the man she's been flirting with online is her husband

The writers that have contributed to this cliché crammed tome have been inventive, entertaining and fervently overzealous in their cliché usage.

Let's hope this book is the first of many.

The stories in this book are presented in the order they were received. Where supplied, the writer's biography appears with their story. I hope you enjoy reading the entertaining tales in this book as much as Jude and I have enjoyed presenting them.

Over and out.

# INTRODUCTION 3

## by Book Aid International

Around the world, millions of people live in a world with few books, or even no books at all. They cannot afford to buy books at home and in schools pupils must share just a few old textbooks. Libraries often offer the best opportunity for people to read, but even libraries often have just a few out of date books. This lack of books leaves children less able to succeed in school, prevents adults from learning throughout their lives and denies people the simple joy of reading.

At Book Aid International we believe that everyone should have access to books that will enrich, improve and change their lives. Every year, we send around one million brand new books a year to libraries, schools, universities, hospitals, refugee camps and prisons where people would otherwise have few opportunities to access books and read. In an average year, these books are read by an estimated 25 million people.

It costs just £2 to send another book, so every penny raised really makes a difference. We would like to thank the contributors and editors of this anthology for their support.

www.bookaid.org

## ACKNOWLEDGMENTS

Big thanks to Flash Fiction Festival Director, Jude Higgins, and all the other festival organisers for helping me unleash the Cliché Challenge upon the planet. You can learn more about the festival here:
www.flashfictionfestival.com

Thanks to David Fielden for designing the cover of this book and building and maintaining my website. Without him, I'd never have created a platform that allowed the writing challenges I run to be so successful. You can learn more about Dave's website building skills at:
www.bluetree.co.uk

Finally, a tritely-worded BIG AS A HOUSE (BY AND LARGE) thank you to everyone who has submitted stories, supported this crazy idea and, in turn, Book Aid International. At the time of writing, we are already well on the way to 100 stories for *Tritely Challenged Volume 2*. Without the support of all the writers who submit their stories, this simply wouldn't be possible.

**TRITELY CHALLENGED**

# 1: A PIECE OF CAKE

## *by Christopher Fielden*

I'm as old as the hills, but can move faster than a speeding bullet.

In the blink of an eye, I have my cake and eat it.

"Harold, you better not be eating my jam sponge. It's for WI." I've heard walls have ears, but eyes?

"Mwmf..." Crumbs spray everywhere.

It's so quiet you could hear a pin drop. I sense Maude getting bent out of shape. Then she appears, as if from nowhere. Caught red handed.

"You've been retired for three weeks, Harold." Maude's voice is as cool as a cucumber. "You're already driving me up the wall. I can't take it anymore. You're a self-centred, selfish old fool."

"That's about the size of it." I have a way with words. I take another bite of sponge.

"That's the icing on the cake. Get out, Harold. You can live in your shed."

I guess that's the way the cookie crumbles.

~

## Christopher Fielden's Biography

Chris writes, runs a humorous short story competition, plays drums and rides his motorcycle, sometimes to Hull. And back again.

He runs many writing challenges and hopes to publish 1,000s of authors in the support of charity.

www.christopherfielden.com

## 2: THE RING OF NEVERARD

### *by Allen Ashley*

Arian, brave neophyte farmhand, and absconding Princess Lealia bowed before the white-haired man in the flowing silver robes.

"Oh mighty Wizard Ganeagle," quoth Arian, "we have fought monsters and dragons and scared scarecrows in this quest."

"And sailed seven seas," Lealia added.

"My children," the wizard replied, "you have done well despite your youth. Truly, I feel that we are winning the battle of Good against Evil. Now, will you faithfully ever-serve your people?"

"Yes, magus," they both responded.

"Then by the sacred prophecy of the ages, I grant you the power of the golden ring of Neverard."

The boy liked this bit, when the wizard set off whizzes, flashes and bangs. But the princess was a year his senior and enquired, "Ganeagle, we have solemnly completed all 12 tasks required on this mission."

"True, my child."

"Then," waving a runic card, "I believe the correct response is: Bingo."

~

# Allen Ashley's Biography

Allen Ashley has been featured many times in the series of writing challenges and hosted the *Sensorially Challenged Volume One* London launch. He is a British Fantasy Award winning editor and works as a creative writing tutor and critical reader.
   www.allenashley.com

# 3: THEY TRIED TO KEEP US APART

## *by Kit de Waal*

"I'll meet you at midnight," he said, then disappeared into thin air.

I watched the clock strike 12, then ran as quick as lightning, slipping and sliding in the sticky mud. Under the silver moonlight, I came to a fork in the road. Which way to turn? I couldn't think straight. My heart was pounding.

He told me he would wait forever, but this would put his love to the test. Then, suddenly, I remembered what he'd whispered in my ear. "Under the old apple tree in the secret garden."

I tiptoed along the narrow path, praying he would be true to his word, and... Yes, I should never have doubted. He grabbed me. We clung together and I pressed my lips to his. Our bodies neared and we became one.

Our black stallions galloped over the fields, taking us away to live happily ever after.

The End.

~

## Kit de Waal's Biography

No author biography supplied.

## 4: A MODERN FAIRYTALE

### *by Marie Gracie*

The grubby urchin boy scratched a living from the dregs of society. Hot tears burnt his cheeks as he cried himself to sleep every night in his run-down hovel.

When he found the prince's shiny new mobile phone, he thought his fortunes might change. He stole through the night to the golden gates of the palace. The flags flapped in the wind and the owls screeched overhead.

At last, finding himself in the golden boy's chamber, the urchin stroked the prince's flaxen hair and waited for the Adonis to stir. It was a rude awakening for the mummy's-boy prince. But smiles cracked across both their faces when the urchin revealed to the prince his lost treasure.

When he came of age, the urchin looked in the mirror and realised he was the woman of the prince's dreams. The wedding went viral and the three of them all lived happily ever after.

~

## Marie Gracie's Biography

After a long and rewarding career in the corporate world, Marie now enjoys writing flash fiction and making abstract paintings, collages and sculpture. She runs courses to encourage others to share her passion for all things creative.

Find Marie on Twitter: @mk161965

# 5: WE'LL CROSS THAT BRIDGE WHEN WE COME TO IT

## *by Valerie Griffin*

Howard cast the hook, line and sinker into the water under the bridge.

Meanwhile, recently retired Neville (who had been told to get out of the house because he was getting under Edna's feet) opened a fresh can of worms. With all due respect to Howard, Neville wished he'd been let off the hook. At this moment in time 'gone fishing' was not his thing.

He pulled out a wriggly worm, but he was fighting a losing battle. The worm turned and fell into the water between a rock and a hard place.

\*

Howard glanced up. With all due respect to Nev, he'd never before thought of him as a sandwich short of a picnic.

"Why don't you take five," he said. "We're obviously not singing off the same hymn sheet here. You know what they say, horses for courses and all that. We'll try bowls next week."

~

## Valerie Griffin's Biography

Valerie lives in Weymouth. She writes fiction with varying success, grows her own weird shaped vegetables, looks after five generations of goldfish and people watches on the seafront. Her first novel is under construction.

Find Valerie on Twitter: @griffin399

# 6: SHE WAS ONLY A BARMAID

## *by Helen Rye*

The tall, handsome surgeon with the flashing blue eyes flicked back his hair as he unfolded his rangy frame from the Lamborghini.

His eyes roamed about the room as he stood on the threshold of the dark, smoky bar. Saving lives was exhausting, but it was his passion, as if he was born to do it. If only his punishing work schedule and dashing good-looks would allow him to find love.

Then their eyes met across the room and it was love at first sight...

\*

Charlene, the blonde and beautiful barmaid, was trying to pursue a singing career, but had yet to hit the big time. As she looked at Dr Rupert from under her enormous eyelashes, she knew she had met her prince and that he would carry her into the sunset like a knight in shining armour.

The End.

~

## Helen Rye's Biography

Helen Rye lives in Norwich and writes fiction on her phone while burning pasta. She has won the Bath Flash Fiction Award, been shortlisted for the Bridport Flash Fiction Prize and is a Best Small Fictions 2017 nominee. 80% biscuits.

Find Helen on Twitter: @helenrye

# 7: GRABBING THE BULL BY THE HORNS

## *by Louise Mangos*

At the Internet Café, we eyed the bottomless pit of photos on the dating site. As sure as Christmas is in July, I knew I'd skip the guy with a face like a blind cobbler's thumb.

Although I'm no spring chicken, I can still cut the mustard. I'd already made a dog's dinner of my first encounter and I couldn't risk opening another can of worms. But I had to get my skates on. I knew Mavis, my blonde-bombshell best buddy, thought she was on the money.

I was hot to trot and, would you believe it, the next hunk I laid my eyes on was the spitting image of George Clooney. In the nick of time, my finger jockeyed for position over the real McCoy and, easy as pie, I hit enter.

~

## Louise Mangos's Biography

Louise is a compulsive writer and drinker of prosecco. She lives on a Swiss Alp with her Kiwi husband and two sons. You can find her on Facebook and Twitter (@LouiseMangos) or visit her website for links to more of her stories:

www.louisemangos.com

## 8: BLOOD, TOIL, SWEAT AND TEARS

### *by Chris Leahy*

At the end of the day, you can't expect people to take you seriously when you've been here all of five minutes. I told that boy, "You might be the gaffer's son, but your father, your grandfather, and his before him, going back as far as anyone can remember – they've all had to learn the same lesson. You listen to old Jack."

Then I explained that the owner doesn't care for anything but his purse. He can afford a few men gone missing in a fall, as long as the coal keeps coming. His daughter is out of reach to common men.

"To be honest," he said, "I don't care, Jack – you were born old and you don't know how things are now. Me and Lizzie – we're going to run away together."

I looked back at him, all the arrogance of his youth, and secretly wished him well, knowing it would end in tears.

~

## Chris Leahy's Biography

No author biography supplied.

## 9: HEARD IT ALL BEFORE

### *by Marcus Robinson*

My eagle-eyes spotted him from afar and I knew he'd be a jobsworth. I bounded down the steps, two at a time, to confront this officious traffic warden who was about to slap a parking ticket onto my sleek and brand spanking new convertible.

"Excuse me," I said, gasping for breath, "but that's my car."

The warden's cold eyes locked with mine. My knees buckled and my pulse quickened as I melted under the intensity of his stare.

"I've only been two minutes," I stammered. "I had to pick up a prescription for my poorly grandmother."

His steely gaze was unrelenting. He must have had ice-water running through his veins. His demeanour was as stiff as his starched collar.

"Have a heart," I pleaded.

He loomed over me as he fixed the ticket to my car's gleaming windscreen.

"I'm sorry, sir," he growled. "But I've heard it all before."

~

## Marcus Robinson's Biography

Marcus Robinson is a freelance writer and editor based in Bristol. Part-time scribbler, full-time procrastinator, he finds it distressingly easy to write flash fiction through the medium of cliché.
   www.linkedin.com/in/marcus-robinson-83907513/

## 10: LOST AT SEA

### *by Christopher Stanley*

"Abandon ship," says Mum, even though we're in the car. Dad's behind the wheel and she's driving him crazy.

"Are we nearly there yet?" I ask.

"Don't get your hopes up," says Mum. "Your father couldn't navigate his way out of a paper bag. Can't see the wood for the trees."

I hate it when she gets her knickers in a twist. Given half a chance, she'll wind him up until the cows come home. Won't let Dad get a word in edgeways. But they'll be all smiles when we arrive. It's like water off a duck's back.

"Might as well be weeing in the wind."

"Watch your tongue," says Dad. In one fluid motion, he unfastens her belt, opens her door and gives her the boot.

"Man overboard," he says, as Mum falls by the wayside.

Luckily, there are plenty of other fish in the sea.

~

## Christopher Stanley's Biography

Christopher Stanley lives in the thick of it with more sons than you can shake a stick at. When the cat's away, he writes like his life depends on it. Follow him to your heart's content.

Find Chris on Twitter: @allthosestrings

## 11: FEMME FATALE

### *by Liz Falkingham*

His office was in a run-down joint in some one-horse town, the beat-up sofa in the corner telling me this wise guy had pushed his wife's buttons once too often.

His craggy face lit up. Who's this sweet deal – an angel with a dirty face, maybe? In a dog-eat-dog world, this puppy was pulling on his heart strings like a cheap balloon.

While he was checking out my ass, I was clocking the safe. Doubt he had me pegged as packing lead, but a girl's gotta have her ace in the hole. When I pulled out my piece, he just lit another cigarette and tipped back his fedora.

"Sweet cheeks," he rasped, "you won't do the crime – lady like you, she can't do the time."

But this broad's no bleeding heart. I shot him anyways – dead men tell no tales.

~

## Liz Falkingham's Biography

Liz Falkingham Temple is a writer based in East Yorkshire. Her work has appeared online and in print, and was shortlisted for the Bath Flash Fiction Prize in 2017. She is currently working on her first novel.

Find Liz on Twitter: @JournoLizF

## 12: THRILL AT THE TILL

### *by Mary Bevan*

Out of the blue, there he was in front of me at the self-checkout. It was love at first sight. Tall, dark and handsome, he towered over me, smiling. Instantly weak at the knees I tipped my shopping basket and groceries cascaded to the floor.

"Can I give you a hand?" His voice was rich and velvety. My stomach turned over.

Stooping to retrieve an errant tomato, his hand brushed mine and our eyes met.

Time stood still.

"How stupid," I muttered, heart pounding, "I can't thank you enough."

"Don't mention it," he said softly, blue eyes twinkling.

If only I could have pulled myself together, got on top of things, who knows where it might have led us. But oh, the unforgiving minute.

"Well, all the best." He straightened up and moved off.

I'd blown it of course, just like that. Life's a bitch. Love hurts – ouch.

~

## Mary Bevan's Biography

Mary writes flash fiction, short stories and poetry. Her pieces have been published in anthologies including *Monday's, Flash Fiction Festival One, This Little World* and *South*. She was long-listed for the 2017 Flash Fiction Prize. She lives in Dorset.

## 13: WHEN IT RAINS, IT POURS

### *by Michelle Konov*

"Abandon ship," sounded across the board, as the kraken sank its fangs into the hull.

The bigger they are, the harder they fall, and the ship keeled over, a fish out of water. It took its final breath in a last-ditch effort – because, hey, you only live once.

"No skin off my back," the chef said, jumping the gun. The kraken was the man (?) of the moment, pulling him under in a jiffy.

"Too many cooks in the kitchen, I guess," a nearby scallywag mouthed off, a short lived laugh escaping before, like clockwork, the kraken pulled the wool over his eyes too.

"Thick as thieves," I heard the lion tamer mumble under his breath. Quick as lightning, he was next.

"Curiosity killed the cat," I sighed, waiting for the other shoe to drop. The kraken left me high and dry. Icing on the cake? The Royal Navy.

~

## Michelle Konov's Biography

Dreamer, writer, winner, quitter. Michelle Konov is a bit of a nerd, kind of a geek, and, well, mostly a dork. English teacher by trade, creative mastermind by nature – save 'creative' and 'mastermind', anyway. Forever filling space with words.

## 14: BAD TO THE BONE

### *by Jo Simmonds*

"Stop getting your knickers in a twist. He might be a vampire, but he gets good grades in biology and have you listened to his flute playing lately?" Scarlett's sarcastic humour was the best thing since sliced bread.

"Yeah... he's a twisted genius."

Sandy sighed heavily. It was raining cats and dogs outside. When it rained it poured. She felt as weak as a kitten.

She could still feel the soreness in her neck from where Michael had sunk his fangs deep. There was something so illicit about the intimacy, especially when he took her over the bonnet of his father's shiny red mustang. The heart-stopping fear led her to the most intense feelings she'd ever experienced in her short life. She was as high as a kite for hours afterwards.

Something glinted in Scarlett's eye, but she was safe here. There was no place like home.

~

## Jo Simmonds' Biography

Jo Simmonds is editor of *The Fiction Pool*. She writes poetry and plays, as well as flash and short stories. She has had fiction published in *The Next Review* and *The Fiction Pool*.

Find Jo on Twitter: @JoCSimmonds

## 15: MUM MAKES A MOUNTAIN OUT OF A MOLEHILL BUT STICKS TO HER GUNS

### by Jill Yates

Mum's a real drama queen, and it really gets up my nose. She makes a big deal of everything, and she's never off my back. Like – when I bunked off school this afternoon.

"Mark my words, you'll rue the day. Idle hands are the devil's playthings. Swanning off after lunch. Words fail me."

"Gimme a break, Mum," I say. "It's just one afternoon." Actually, that's a porky.

"Which is one too many. You've got to knuckle down. Your school marks don't set the world on fire. You promised you'd turn over a new leaf and pull your finger out."

"I will. Tomorrow."

"I've heard that before. Pull the other one."

I was bored out of my skull, so tried changing tack.

"Mum, I'm starving. I could eat a horse. Any chance of some grub?"

"You are pushing your luck. In your dreams, sunshine."

Oh well. Nothing ventured, nothing gained.

~

## Jill Yates' Biography

Jill Yates lives in Oxfordshire. She has written five pantomimes for village performance, a children's novel and has an adult novel in work. She has more recently taken up short story writing and has already won one major prize.

# 16: ALONE AND MISUNDERSTOOD, HE SUFFERS FOR HIS ART

## *by JY Saville*

Up at the crack of dawn, he pored over his manuscript with a fine toothcomb, wielding a pencil red as the blood he'd sweated over it. Rain streaked the window and the meagre fire in his attic room burned rejection slips: close, but no cigar. He was tearing his hair out, plumbing the depths of his soul, but his muse had abandoned him.

His last story sold for a pittance, barely buying a crust of bread. It was the last story about… Her. He'd worshipped her from afar – it was love at first sight – but she barely knew he existed, looked right through him in the street.

He'd reached the end of his tether. Eviction was on the cards. He tied his bedsheet noose, crying out to the cruel gods. A knock rang out and she stood on the threshold, eyes brimming with tears. He hung his head in shame.

~

## JY Saville's Biography

JY Saville writes stories of various lengths and genres, including some at *The Fiction Pool*, *Firefly* magazine, and forthcoming in *Confingo*.
  www.thousandmonkeys.wordpress.com

## 17: THE GATHERING STORM

*by Ville Nummenpää*

That night he had a dream. In the dream, all the previously mentioned incidents in the story seemed to merge into an unconvincing montage that filled up a page and a half.

Mr Evil was holding his wife, kids, mum, girlfriend and Spotty as captives, and was holding a giant bomb above their heads. The fuse was lit.

"You and I are not so different. We are just on opposite sides," Mr Evil said.

"No," Goodguy tried to scream, but couldn't.

"This is the first day of the rest of your life. See you in hell," Mr Evil said, and pressed the button. Then everything was engulfed in flames.

"Noooo..."

Then he woke up in a cold sweat and noticed an item on his bedside table, handed to him earlier in the dream, thus leaving him wondering, *Was it a dream after all?*

~

## Ville Nummenpää's Biography

Ville is a screenwriter/playwright from Finland. He writes short stories for fun, and gets something published on occasion. The only thing he takes seriously is humour.

## 18: CAPTAIN CLICHÉ –VS– THE MIXED-METAPHOR MATADOR (FINAL SHOWDOWN)

*by Mike Scott Thomson*

High noon at the old saloon. With bated breath, I await my archenemy.

The very thought of him makes my skin crawl.

I spot him a mile off. Too late to turn on my heels now. I must stand my ground.

Next thing I know, we're eye to eye.

I get the ball rolling.

"This town ain't big enough for the both of us," I sneer.

"Take a running hike," he spits. "I'll shoot the wind out of your saddle."

There's a deafening silence. And then it dawns on me:

He's as weak as a newborn baby.

And I'm shaking like a leaf.

I indicate the bar. "How about some Dutch courage?"

He smirks. "You can read me like the back of your hand."

\*

Two hours later, we're as thick as skunks.

No – as drunk as thieves.

Hic.

Safe to say, we've wiped the slate clean.

~

## Mike Scott Thomson's Biography

Mike Scott Thomson's short stories have been published by journals, anthologies and have won the occasional award, including first prize in Chris Fielden's inaugural To Hull And Back competition.

Based in south London, he works in broadcasting.

www.mikescottthomson.com

## 19: TAKEN TO THE CLEANERS

### *by Michael Rumsey*

Normally we have a run of the mill business and everything is hunky-dory, but once in a blue moon we get a special request.

Last week, a dozen robes from the local monastery. It goes without saying we were happy to oblige, but if it's not one thing it's another. Three quarters needed patching. Easier said than done, but we had to face up to the facts. It would be far and away best to cut the cloth to suit, no half measures and a stitch in time saves nine. Could we also dry clean and re-colour in two shades? Six of one half a dozen of the other.

Soon, all was cut and dried, but the robes came out stiff. To put it in a nutshell, we are older and wiser and it stands to reason we now realise old habits dye hard.

~

## Michael Rumsey's Biography

Perhaps it is more by luck than judgement, that Michael's 150th short piece has just been published. Asked why he concentrates on flash fiction, he claims to be a man of few words.

www.facebook.com/mrumsey

## 20: GENERAL MONTGOMERY'S ADDRESS TO THE TROOPS BEFORE D-DAY (AS I REMEMBER IT)

*by John Notley*

"Now, chaps, we have a tough job ahead of us. This is the calm before the storm. With our backs to the wall, if we stand united, putting our best foot forward, keeping our noses clean with a stiff upper lip and, thinking of King and country, we will triumph against all odds.

"The Hun is already counting his chickens and will stop at nothing. But we can be sure they have some dirty tricks up their sleeves. We are made of much sterner stuff and they are no match for us. It will be a long and dusty road, but Rome wasn't built in a day. The first step is the hardest but, if we all pull together, not looking over our shoulders, leaving no stone unturned, we can bring peace in our time and earn our place in history. Up boys and at 'em."

~

## John Notley's Biography

John, a retired travel agent, having failed to make his fortune has taken up his pen again hoping to redress the situation. He had a few stories and poems published some years ago but feels it's time to hit the jackpot.

www.linkedin.com/in/john-notley-503666102/

## 21: FROM ZERO TO HERO

### *by Helen Combe*

A detective's lot is not a happy one. The wife left me when I fell off the wagon. I've just handed in my gun and badge and I'm now getting drunk in a strip joint.

I'd shot the guy six times, then I stepped out for a fag and he did a Lazarus, leaped up, killed three people, then dropped dead again and I got the blame.

I've been suspended, but an old dog can't learn new tricks.

I need my job back.

Then I hear the ticking from behind the bar and I see it. I remember my bomb disposal training in 'Nam. I get out my penknife. Red wire or black wire? I decide to cut black, then, at the last minute, I change my mind and cut red. The timer stops at 001.

I'm the stuff heroes are made of. I'll be welcomed back into the fold.

~

## Helen Combe's Biography

Helen started writing in earnest in 2009 after joining the Solihull Writers. She was shortlisted for the *To Hull And Back Anthology 2016*. Previous hobbies include belly dance, medieval re-enactment and being voted Supreme Ruler of the Universe.

www.facebook.com/HelenCombeWriter/

## 22: A NIGHT OUT INTO THE UNFORGETABLE

### *by Sandra Orellana*

The old story – the fear of falling in love. I lost track of time. I had the time of my life. I danced all night... The next morning, I woke up dazed, without a care in the world.

Scared out of my wits, but brave as a lion, I got up and warmed my coffee. I asked myself, as weak as a kitten, if the dance lasted an eternity, where could it go? Could I live happily ever after?

I became as strong as an ox, full of life, and snapped out of it. I answered myself with good spirits. It won't go anywhere. So I just served my coffee. I'm as old as the hills, but I still went out to dance all night. I lost track of time, but I stopped and asked myself again – why do I dance, if I don't care to dance?

~

## Sandra Orellana's Biography

Sandra Orellana is the author of *The Arch Of Surprises*.

She enjoys writing short stories for Christopher Fielden. She is promoting her children's book and working on her second novel. She's an American living in Mexico City and San Miguel Allende.

www.amazon.com/Arch-Surprises-Sandra-Orellana/dp/1983552658/

## 23: FOLLOW YOUR HEART

*by Helen Fawdon-Rochester*

Bide your time, as good things come to those who wait. These words echoed through Edna's head while she got ready to go on her date. Dressed to the nines, despite being as poor as a church mouse, she had managed to rob Peter to pay Paul and buy an outfit.

Edna was on cloud nine. It was full steam ahead to meet Thomas. Thomas was as fit as a fiddle for his age and, despite his checkered past, Edna knew that beggars could not be choosers at her age. Therefore, she decided to follow her heart and accept Thomas's offer of becoming his blushing bride.

~

## Helen Fawdon-Rochester's Biography

Helen Fawdon-Rochester lives in North Northumberland with her Labrador dog and her elderly cat. She enjoys reading and creative writing.

## 24: ONE LAST JOB TO PAY FOR HIS DAUGHTER'S OPERATION (HE WISHES HE'D BEEN THERE FOR HER WHEN SHE WAS YOUNG)

*by Robert Barrett*

Reggie's gnarled and grizzled hands clutched the gun to his bosom. It was hot as hell and the fat bank teller with the glasses lost his nerve and pressed the panic button. Reggie looked him straight in the eye and told him to put the money in the bag. Sirens rang in the distance. Reggie was sweating like a pig. He took the money and ran, just in time to see the getaway car vanish into thin air.

Down the street, in a cloud of dust, a phalanx of cop cars were screaming towards him. The sun was beating down on his head. He pulled out his phone and punched in his daughter's number.

"Sorry I wasn't a better father. Your mum and I, we got married in a fever and, at the end of the day, when the dust settled, we just couldn't see the wood for the trees."

~

## Robert Barrett's Biography

Robert Barrett lives in Co. Wicklow, Ireland. He writes flash fiction, short stories and plays and was the winner of the 2017 PJ O'Connor Awards for radio drama.

Find Robert on Twitter: @barrettrob

## 25: ALL AT SEA

*by Dawn Ovington*

We had been like two peas in a pod, but had drifted apart. The regatta was in full flow and she needed me to compete. It was all hands on deck. Her new boyfriend, the captain, looked me up and down and shrugged. "Any port in a storm, I guess."

We set sail with the wind at our backs and glided over the waves. By nightfall, the tide had turned. We bobbed on the ebb and flow of the tide. It was the calm before the storm. The sky opened, the thunder rolled and the lightning flashed. The mainsail was hit and split in two. It was all lost at sea. In the panic, she called my name and I ran to her. I told her everything was going to be alright. She pulled the cord to light the flare, but the spark was gone.

~

## Dawn Ovington's Biography

Dawn Ovington teaches small humans for money. She would do it for free, but then she couldn't afford to heat her home in the Wicklow Mountains, where winter lasts six months. Her favourite season is summer.

## 26: ACCIDENTAL LOVERS

### *by Juno Grace*

College was new to her and she didn't know what to expect. A tall handsome stranger walked by and bumped into her by accident. They both dropped all their books and said, "I'm so sorry," in unison. They looked up and their eyes met. They were frozen like a rabbit in the headlights. It was as if time had stood still.

She knew that this was true love. He helped her pick up her books and, as it turned out, they were all in the same classes. That summer, they took their true love vows.

"We live 5,000 miles apart," she said.

"Don't worry my darling," he said.

"But we are from different socio-economic backgrounds," she said.

"Love will find a way," he said.

"You're right, nothing on Earth can keep us apart," she said.

They built a home for themselves, had three kids and a dog.

~

## Juno Grace's Biography

Juno Grace is 14 years old. She is a secret agent currently working undercover as a schoolgirl. She enjoys writing, reading and secret-agenting.

## 27: SEIZE THE DAY

### *by Alan Barker*

At the crossroads of my stage career, I felt this show must go on. Being a matinee stand-in, I had no axe to grind with Max, the actor who, yet again, phoned in sick.

"You know which way the wind blows here," said Jill, the stage manager. "Perform or sling your hook."

I didn't want to turn the tables on Max, but every dog has its day, and this was mine. I had to strike while the iron was hot as he who hesitates is lost.

What a turn up for the books. In two shakes of a lamb's tail, I was on stage dressed to the nines.

*Que Sera, Sera*, I thought.

When Max returned, as fit as a fiddle, we came eyeball to eyeball, while he had to face the music and eat humble pie.

I said to him, "As you sow, so must you reap."

~

## Alan Barker's Biography

I live in what was once a Roman fortress, in South Wales. The many stories and legends connected with it inspire my passion for writing short stories, plays, poems and my first novella, *Splash Point*, set in Rome.

Find Alan on Twitter: @italisalute

## 28: LET IT GO

### *by Glen Donaldson*

"You're as cold as ice," said Hans, who was not happy at all.

Always willing to take a metaphor and run with it, Anna shot back with a barely concealed look of frost, "And you're skating on it."

"Doesn't cut any ice with me, petal," he bellowed, the veins in his neck beginning to turn eggplant purple. "You gotta bad attitude and, as Uncle Glorbert always used to say, 'Bad attitudes are like flat tyres'. You ain't goin' anywhere 'til ya change it, especially in this weather."

Amateur psychoanalysis had always been one of Anna's pet peeves, but she knew the combined character flaws just exchanged as insults between them were merely the tip of the iceberg. For the moment at least, she'd put their disagreements on ice and allow Hans to think he'd had the final word. A foil-wrapped fruitcake would be their makeup totem later that afternoon.

~

## Glen Donaldson's Biography

Glen Donaldson knows it takes two mystery writers to fit a lightbulb – one to screw the bulb almost all the way in and the other to give a surprising twist at the end.
www.goosefleshsite.wordpress.com

## 29: THE PRIME MINISTER'S SPEECH
## OR
## WHAT A ROOMFUL OF MONKEYS WITH LAPTOPS CHURNED OUT

*by Tracy Lee-Newman*

"Let me be perfectly frank. The facts are that, across the board, our long-term economic plan of opportunity for all and steady growth, is moving Britain forward. But clearly, up and down the country, hard-working families are at a crossroads. And may I make this point? Let's not forget that we inherited a raft of problems from the previous administration and, so, whilst the squeezed middle is obviously safe in our hands, there is still much to do. However, with my party in the driving seat, we will deliver on our strong and stable plan to make this country fit for purpose in the modern global era. On that, you have my cast iron guarantee."

~

## Tracy Lee-Newman's Biography

No author biography supplied.

## 30: CUT TO THE QUICK

### by Lesley Anne Truchet

"He's as weak as a kitten," Dr Goode remarked.

"Nonsense, man, you're as blind as a bat if you think that."

Dr Goode bridled. "He's as old as the hills. He needed a vasectomy like I need tits."

"I told him that, he's as stubborn as a mule. Anyway, if he wants to be as daft as a brush I make a fast buck," Dr Badd chortled.

"Thanks to you, he could soon be as dead as a dodo and pushing up daisies, then what? That'll put the cat amongst the pigeons." Dr Goode waved his stethoscope to emphasise his words.

"Don't get your knickers in a twist. He'll be as fit as a fiddle in a few days."

"I should shop you for malpractice."

"What malpractice? He just gave his wife another bun in the oven."

Dr Goode didn't respond.

"Cat got your tongue then?"

~

## Lesley Anne Truchet's Biography

Lesley Truchet has been writing for several years and has a number of short stories, articles and poems published on paper and on the internet. She is currently writing her first novel.

# 31: MY LITTLE AUNT LUCY

## *by Dorothy Snelson*

She's as bright as a button. No flies on Auntie. She may be 102 'not out', as she likes to say, but she's all her chairs at home.

We're awaiting the Home Librarian.

"That Marjorie's like the side of a house," Auntie says. "She must eat like a horse. Voice like a foghorn. You'll hear her before you see her. At least she's not got a face like a wet weekend. Not like that Job's Comforter Maureen, the care assistant. She's every ailment under the sun, to hear her talk, and some that haven't been invented yet."

"You're a card, Auntie," I say. "Naughty but nice."

"Bit like that Alan Titchmarsh's books Marjorie's bringing. There's more to him than his petunias. He's a dark horse, that one."

Outside there's a *crash, bang, wallop*.

"Butter-fingers has dropped the books again," grins Auntie.

~

## Dorothy Snelson's Biography

No author biography supplied.

## 32: HAPPILY

### by Len Saculla

"After their big adventure in the woods, the boy and the girl moved back into the little cottage with the thatched roof and lived happily ever after."

"What did they do in the rest of their lives, Mummy?"

"Oh, they probably grew up and found some work and likely got married and had children. A girl as quiet as a mouse and a boy as strong as an ox."

"And was the dragon really gone?"

"It said: 'His fire was put out like a light.'"

"And the witch?"

"As dead as a dodo."

"I liked this story, Mummy. Next time can we have *The Shining*?"

"Only if you behave sensibly at Auntie May's ninetieth birthday party tomorrow."

"Promise. I'll be as good as gold."

~

## Len Saculla's Biography

To his astonishment, Len Saculla has once been a Pushcart Prize nominee. He has recently been published at Speculative 66 (USA online SF and horror magazine). He has also featured in Christopher Fielden's adverb, sensory, nonsensical and preposition challenges.

## 33: THE COURSE OF TRUE LOVE

### *by Paul Garratt*

We were made for each other, but there was an elephant in the room. I was a mere duck farmer and she was the squire's daughter. When push came to shove he forbade the match.

The chickens had come home to roost and left me with egg on my face. I was at the end of my tether.

I threw myself into my work. I'd trained my ducks to follow me like sheep and led them to the village market two by two.

Later that day there was a knock at the door. It was the squire and his daughter.

The squire didn't stand on ceremony. "I admire a man who gets all his ducks in a row. You can have my daughter's hand."

Her smile lit up the room and I was as pleased as punch. We would live happily ever after. Every cloud has a silver lining.

~

## Paul Garratt's Biography

Paul Garratt lives in Swindon, but don't feel sorry for him as it's not as bad as people make out.

He writes right-handed, plays darts left-handed and would like to be better at both.

Find Paul on Twitter: @PaulG258

## 34: THE YOUNG DUKE AND THE COMELY MAID

*by Catherine Assheton-Stones*

The handsome young Duke Ferdinand rode into town on his glossy black stallion. He stopped at an inn where a buxom wench serving ale caught his eye. Her cheeks dimpled prettily under his warm gaze.

He took to visiting the inn every evening, passing the time of day, exchanging pleasantries with the comely servant girl. He wasn't her only admirer: Davith, the cruel but lumbering oaf who helped in the stable cast secret lustful glances at her.

Finding the inn empty one night, young Ferdinand strolled into the yard to look for the wench. He found her trembling, about to be molested, pinned against the wall by Davith's sinewy arms.

"Unhand this lady," he cried, flinging Davith to the ground.

As the spurned suitor crawled away, the young duke took the maid tenderly in his arms. She lay half swooning, but very willing, while he kissed her tears away.

~

## Catherine Assheton-Stones' Biography

Catherine Assheton-Stones has short stories published in the second Stories for Homes anthology and the online literary magazine STORGY. She's also writes book and film reviews. She's lived in many different places and hopes to continue exploring.

Find Catherine on Twitter: @CatherineAsshet

# 35: WORDS ARE CHEAP

## *by Jonathan Heriz-Smith*

To cut a long story short, I met my Waterloo the other day. The long and the short of it is, in a nutshell, that I've been playing a mug's game. They say blood is thicker than water, but it's nowhere as thick as my sister. Let's just say if you give her an inch she'll take a mile, and then some.

What happened was, I lent her a tenner and she turned on her heel and headed for the hills, leaving me lost for words. Trying to get it back was like getting blood from a stone – I was banging my head against a brick wall, and I could tear my hair out. This was literally the last straw in the rollercoaster of our friendship. I could wait until the cows came home, but a leopard can't change its spots, so I kissed her and that tenner goodbye.

~

## Jonathan Heriz-Smith's Biography

Johnny is a counsellor, architect and writer. He recently performed his Brexit poem 'Headless Chickens and the Elephant in the Room' at the Wells Literature Festival. He is currently writing a historical novel set in Cornwall between the two world wars.

## 36: MURDER ON THE HOOF

*by Lesley McLaren*

"Dead as a doornail," boomed Dr Jubilus, before Inspector Choler could jump the gun.

The young woman's mutilated body was naked as a babe.

Choler groaned as he crouched beside the pathologist. 11 roof murders in 20 minutes, not counting advert breaks, had turned his shift into a hard night on the tiles; his knees were killing him. Dog-tired, he raked a hand through his hair while Jubilus inserted a probe into the victim's accusing eyeball.

"Frenzied attack, Inspector."

A sight for sore eyes. "Weapon?"

"Blunt instrument."

"Time of death?"

The doc's old-fashioned look was par for the course. "Fancy a pint?"

Swallowing bile, Choler shook his head. Beer made him sick as a dog. Besides, he'd better hotfoot it, if more than Trudy here were to meet their maker tonight. Yeah, he knew Trudy.

Choler knew all his victims like the back of his hand.

~

## Lesley McLaren's Biography

Lesley McLaren lives in the French Mediterranean Pyrenees. Wild walks with her bonkers dog in them there mountains fire her imagination for rollicking yarns about all sorts of stuff, but they also light her fire for writing about nature.
www.mediterraneanpyrenees.com

## 37: X'GGORRT'TH OF K'ZAGATH-AED

*by Vyvien R. R. Beauxchamps*

One hand on his mace, X'ggorrt'th of the K'zagath-Aed dwarves surveyed the distant tower, for his quest was at its dawning. Red hair billoweth.

"Argh," he shouted. Mead sloshed over the edge of his tankard. "Away with us, to save the princess." And as with one heavy boot the motley lot was a-march. Shields and spears jabbed the air and the band uttered a war song that did echo from the mountains.

Any many beasts did they slay in their path; the feared Wyrme of that bygone age; the Auk who snatched many of X'ggorrt'th's kin, prompting gnashings of teeth before an arrow pierced its heart, 'til ere long this intrepid company arrived at the tower only to learn that the princess was happy, and did not desire the society of dwarves, and that they could keep their ale and their obsession with subterranean riches and that they had best leave.

~

## Vyvien R. R. Beauxchamps' Biography

No author biography supplied.

## 38: THE DEAD PARROT

### *by John S Alty*

Taking the stairs in leaps and bounds he landed on his feet. Then he saw it. A dead parrot. It was in the dead centre of the small but perfectly formed room. Eyes like a hawk, he scanned for clues and on the scrubbed kitchen table were four candles. No, not four candles. Fork handles.

His aging but still active mother worked her fingers to the bone getting them to market to put food on the table to feed the hungry mouths because the buck stopped with her. But that's another story.

When the dust had settled it was plain as a pike-staff that all was not right with the world. It was a different story now.

"I've asked you to assemble in the parlour to tell you that the butler did it," said the inspector, pointing to each of them with his pipe.

~

## John S Alty's Biography

John Alty has travelled extensively and has lived in Hong Kong, South Africa, USA and Canada. He now lives in the UK and writes for the pleasure of it. He has been published in various magazines.

Find John on Twitter: @JohnSaltyjohn

# 39: LAST DAY AT THE OFFICE

## *by Margaret Edwards*

"We have to let you go, Norman. Our feathered friends have finally come home to roost and the excrement's hit the fan. Stinks to high heaven."

"Yes," I admit wretchedly. "That's the elephant in the room."

So, goodbye blue sky thinking, it's raining on my parade with no rainbow's end, no golden handshake. Annoyingly, I had seen it coming. When you wake up hungover on the wrong side of the bed between a rock and a hard place, suddenly you're falling between two stools and shooting yourself in the foot.

"Don't get me started on the elephant," he growls. "Though, to be fair, he's alone in shifting more ordure than he creates."

There's nothing to lose now. "OK, at this moment in time maybe you're the fat cat. But when I'm a rich and famous author, I'll not only be the cat with the cream, but the cream-smothered cat's pyjamas."

~

## Margaret Edwards' Biography

Writer from age seven, until thirty-year gap for absorbing family and job. Now work-free and urgently trying to make up for lost time. Minor poetry prizes and publication, now infatuated with the Short Story but still grovelling in shortlist anterooms.

## 40: HELL HATH NO FURY

### *by Rose Farris*

The Sweeney Tod were off like a shot, siren wailing like a banshee.

"You're late to the party," said the Governor. "She's stiff as a board. Yet another innocent victim of the Acton Mauler."

"Mark my words, we won't rest until we've banged up this villain," snarled DI Grabber, chain smoking furiously.

"I'll round up the usual suspects, boss," chirped his sidekick, plucky rookie Sally Tryer.

Back at the station, all hell broke loose as hardened criminals by the dozen were herded into holding cells. All of a sudden, a brassy blonde burst in like a bat out of hell. "Eric Bodger," she shrieked. "How could you two-time me after all these years? Here you are, Inspector. Eric's diary, with all the gory details of his murder spree."

"We've got the Acton Mauler bang to rights and no mistake," chortled Grabber. "Come on, Tryer, let's go down the pub."

~

## Rose Farris's Biography

Rose Farris writes short fiction about any random subject that pops into her head. Having exhausted the patience of family and friends, she now aspires to gain a wider audience for her (usually slightly grim) stories.

# 41: A GLASGOW STORY

## *by Margaret Duffy*

See ma man, he's a total bevvy merchant. Ah took the bull by the horns on Friday and tore a strip aff him for coming in wi' a face like a weel skelped arse and falling down, steaming, in the blink of an eye. Waste of time, could shout till the cows come home. Been like that since the weans flew the nest. Actually, basically, that's a pile o' turd, we've never sung frae the same hymn sheet, no' even frae the same book. Shotgun wedding it was, me up the spout, bun in the oven, him legless from the start.

    Still cannae get ma heid round it, but. At the end of the day, ahm as fit as a fiddle, always look on the bright side and think every cloud has a silver lining, and he's at the boozers again, gettin' rat arsed.

~

## Margaret Duffy's Biography

I am a Glaswegian widow who writes crime novels and short stories. Unfortunately, nothing published yet, though I was longlisted for the Mslexia Novel Comp in 2015. I'm still working on the second novel.

## 42: SMELL THE ROSES

*by Jamie Graham*

Jeanette needed a hobby, but lacked self-confidence. Her hair was neglected, her clothes functional and, sadly, she was well aware she was no oil painting. Jonathan was still denying his affair with Celia, his secretary.

The garden was her only solace. While Jonathan was having his wicked way with that floosy, she was on her ageing knees, pulling up weeds.

One fine summer's evening, with the temperature still hot, a muscly young man pulled up in a van. He had a Mediterranean look about him and an accent to die for.

Jeanette's Christmases had all come at once. After she'd watched him mow the lawn, they threw caution to the wind and made sweet love before he'd even emptied the cuttings.

Jeanette basked in the smell of the roses as she got to her feet and watched the gardener drive off into the sunset.

~

## Jamie Graham's Biography

Jamie Graham is a Scottish writer and *Seinfeld* fan on the wrong side of 40. Follow his flash fiction ramblings on Twitter: @jgrahamwriter

## 43: IT WAS ALL A DREAM

*by Claudie Whitaker*

Dave went from bad to worse after that run-in with the bloke at the petrol station.

"I'm not even joking," I ejaculated. "Do that again, you're history."

Dave looked down in the dumps, but he knew the way to my heart, when he really thought about it.

"So. How about Harry Potter World?"

It felt like a breakthrough moment. To be honest, I was sceptical, but didn't want to rock the boat.

So. En route to HP World, we stop for petrol. Dave fills up, goes inside to pay. Suddenly, I know something's wrong. I can feel it in my bones. Quick as lightning, I undo my seatbelt. Then the whole place blows. Black fire billows towards me.

I open my eyes. Thank goodness, lovely Dave's snug as a bug in a rug beside me in bed.

How could I ever have doubted him?

~

## Claudie Whitaker's Biography

No author biography supplied.

## 44: THE NEVER ENDING STORY

### *by Sandra Phillips*

Unaccustomed as I am to public speaking, I feel I must say a few words about the bride and groom. I am honoured to act as best man.

Kevin and I have been best friends since primary school and I love him like a brother. He was always the best at everything, student and worker. I could say he is as good as gold and worth his weight in gold.

Cheryl came along with eyes as blue as the sky and he was hooked. She found his love as easy as taking candy from a baby. Their marriage was a foregone conclusion, and may their days ahead be as clear as the light at the end of a tunnel.

I thank you now to be all upstanding and wish the bride and groom all the luck in the world.

(Aside) They're certainly going to need it.

~

## Sandra Phillips' Biography

My book, *The Narrow Doorway*, about psychic activities, is available on Amazon. I write articles and have poems in many anthologies.

I belong to the Enfield Poets and attend sessions with Allen Ashley. I especially enjoyed reading poetry to jazz.

## 45: NILS AND JUNE

### *by Jude Higgins*

Nils, flinty good looks, tweedy Mogg jacket, scowled balefully at June.

"Nobody said our relationship was going to be a rose garden," he growled.

"I never thought it would be a walk in the park," June whispered. Nils's cut-glass accent and manly chest had always been her downfall. But now he loomed over her.

"You make my blood boil," he said through clenched teeth. "Why must you always agree?"

Thoughts of a nice black pudding raced through her head. Her dad had made it at the butcher's shop. To help, she'd often set a pot of pig's blood on the stove, watched it bubble. Tears welled in her eyes at the memory.

Nils melted. He never could abide a woman crying. And now he was entranced once more.

"Your eyes are like pools," he said.

"Hidden depths," she replied as he folded her into his arms.

~

## Jude Higgins' Biography

Jude Higgins is a writer of short fiction, published widely in magazines and anthologies. Her chapbook *The Chemist's House* was published by V.Press in 2017. She organises Bath Flash Fiction Award and directs Flash Fiction Festivals, UK.

www.judehiggins.com

# 46: NOT EVERY CLOUD...

## *by Marion Turner*

It was like hitting your head against a brick wall, talking to the boss. No amount of 'giving it a 110%' could make a silk purse out of a sow's ear, not in a million years. The job was doomed to failure and we might as well have called it a day right then. In fact, I'd have eaten my hat if anyone had an inkling of how to solve the problem. We were in dire straits.

"A glass half-empty, that's your problem," he'd said. "Believe in yourself. Put some lead in your pencil, man, and get weaving."

"He's a victim of his own success, the boss," said Joe. "Thinks he's Jesus Christ. Well we'll need a miracle to sort this one out."

We worked our socks off all night and by morning could've eaten a scabby horse.

And it had still all gone belly up.

~

## Marion Turner's Biography

Marion writes poetry and short stories. Recently, her poem 'Magnolias' appeared in *The Four Seasons* anthology by Kind of a Hurricane Press, whilst 'The Old Curiosity Shop', a short story, was published in *Tales Magazine*.

## 47: CHEWING THE CUD

*by Lynn-Marie Harper*

"Take me back to childhood," the psychotherapist said.

"It was as green as the grass," the girl answered.

"What the hell does that mean?" he asked.

"We lived in seventh heaven most of the time, floating our boats downriver. School was right up my street, I took to it like a duck to water. Well, it was the cornerstone of my existence, in the way of the world sense. The teachers called me bold as brass, although science turned into a prison of my own making."

"And what was home like?" he asked.

Cool as a cucumber she turned her eyes heavenward. "Well, apart from my yellow belly of a brother, it was hunky-dory, as ordered as apple pie." And then, like the cat that got the cream and in a voice as loud as thunder, she roared into a rousing chorus of 'Whip Crack Away'.

~

## Lynn-Marie Harper's Biography

Lynn-Marie writes mainly poetry, with sorties into life writing and fiction, and has been published in print and online publications. She lives in London and has most recently worked in libraries and read to hospice patients for several years.

www.miralinka1.wordpress.com

## 48: UNDER THE BED

### by Sandra Unerman

"You never ever listen to me. Last night, as soon as you left me alone, the monster crept out from under the bed and ate my fingernails. It's coming back tonight for the rest of me."

"I don't want to hear any more made-up maunderings. You're old enough to live in the real world now. And stop biting your nails."

"I don't bite them. The monster ate them. Tasty as toasted cheese, he said they were. And he licked his lips over the treat he's saving for tonight."

"Don't be ridiculous. I've no sympathy with this nonsense. Goodnight."

"Leave the light on, please, Mum."

"Certainly not. Do you think electricity grows on trees? I'm going."

Out with the light. From under the bed slips the tip of a tail and a claw. Who can run faster, boy or monster?

~

## Sandra Unerman's Biography

Sandra Unerman is a fantasy writer who lives in London and is a member of London Clockhouse Writers. Her novels *Spellhaven* and *Ghosts and Exiles* are available from Mirror World Publishing.

www.sandraunermanwriter.com

## 49: FIRST ITEM ON THE AGENDA

### *by Ejder S. Raif*

"Get a move on."

Mr Tibbs' voice bellowed around the hall as loud as thunder, making the staff jump out of their skin as they helped to set up for the Annual General Meeting. There wasn't long to go.

Everyone was under pressure – except for Danny, who was as cool as a cucumber. They thought it was rather odd.

"Annual General Meetings are boring," said Lesley, miserably.

"Tell me about it," said Sam. "I'll be as happy as Larry when it's all over."

"I don't know how Danny can be so calm," said Lesley.

"And I don't know how Grace can be as quiet as a mouse," said Sam, referring to his timid colleague who was busy preparing the refreshments.

Mr Tibbs sat down, shaking his head as everyone worked their socks off. He felt like he wasn't getting any younger.

~

# Ejder S. Raif's Biography

Ejder has been published in Issue 2 of *Boscombe Revolution*, NUHA Foundation's 2013 Blogging Prizes, *Adverbially Challenged Volume 1*, *Nonsensically Challenged Volume 1* and *Sensorially Challenged Volume 1*. He lives in London and works as a Student Support Worker.

## 50: A FAREWELL KISS

### *by C.I. Selkirk*

Faster than a speeding bullet,
   In the blink of an eye,
   Like a runaway train,
   He soared like an eagle towards his destiny, the damsel in distress.
   She was shaking like a leaf,
   Standing in a pool of light.
   It was love at first sight.
   "My hero," she whispered.
   He swept her off her feet. She was light as a feather. She gazed at his rugged good looks in the mask. He lost himself in the deep blue pools of her eyes. Beauty was in the eye of the beholder.
   Her lips, soft as pillows,
   Smooth as silk,
   Red as rubies,
   Brushed his.
   "You must keep my identity a secret," he said. "For your own safety."
   He slumped to the floor like a tonne of bricks.
   She wiped the poison off her lips.
   He coulda been a contender, but she was just too much woman for him.

~

## C.I. Selkirk's Biography

No author biography supplied.

## 51: GAËL CLICHY'S CLICHÉD CAREER CHOICES

*by Martin Strike*

Gaël Clichy has parted company with Manchester City, taking his chances with his playing career in Istanbul.

The star joined Arsenal in 2003. As luck would have it, he found himself left back in the changing room, playing second fiddle to Ashley Cole. When Cole left in bad blood, Clichy made the position his own until, in his pomp and despite the best laid plans of mice and men, a recurring back injury proved his Achilles' heel and sent him back to square one.

Back at the drawing board, with his injured back against the wall, he rolled his sleeves up and got back in the saddle, eventually catching the eye of high-flying city who bent over backwards and paid top dollar to secure his services.

Six years on and past his prime, Clichy has called it a day and transferred to new horizons in Turkey.

~

## Martin Strike's Biography

Football provides 101 times more headroom for cliché than most ball games. Martin is sick as a parrot about this and holds no truck with this Gallic player, nor either of the English teams referred to. He does, however, enjoy a fine turkey dinner during which he laments the change to Istanbul from the more evocatively named, Constantinople.

## 52: LIGHT AT THE END OF THE TUNNEL

### *by Helena Boland*

Nuala was caught between a rock and a hard place. Her father was making a match for her with the largest farmer in these parts. She, having just finished school, was as green as grass.

Her father said that a man who was here today and gone tomorrow was worse than no man at all. Nuala could not see the wood for the trees.

\*

Willie worked his socks off to make ends meet, supporting Josephine, his invalid sister. Josephine was as bitter as a lemon, sitting in her wheelchair, and Willie knew in his heart of hearts that he needed a young woman.

Cool as a cucumber, he entered the kitchen.

"Won't you sit down and have a cup of tea," Nuala chanted.

Sitting across the table sipping his tea, it became clear as day to Willie that they could be like two peas in a pod.

It was his chance.

~

## Helena Boland's Biography

No author biography supplied.

# 53: TAKEN FOR A RIDE

## *by Sivan Pillai*

I should have smelled a rat when the house was offered dirt cheap. Instead, I was in the seventh heaven and bought it without a second thought.

Soon, the cat was out of the bag: it was a haunted house.

I wanted to drop it like a hot potato. My 'friends' promised to help.

I was pleased as Punch when one Hubert called me to have a tête-à-tête about the property. Though well after sundown, he insisted that I meet him at his home in a jiffy.

I reached the spot on the double. The house was pitch dark and quiet as a mouse. My knocks went unheeded.

A light tap on my shoulder made me jump out of my skin. A man, as thin as air, stood measuring me, suspicious as a cat.

"Wanted to meet Hubert," I blurted out.

"Hubert?" he squealed. "He kicked the bucket years ago."

~

# Sivan Pillai's Biography

Sivan Pillai is a retired professor of English from Navsari Agricultural University, India. He lives in Navsari.

Find Sivan on Twitter: @sivan_pillai

## 54: NO PAIN NO GAIN

### *by Céline Samson*

I can't believe what's happened to me. I've fallen head over heels for my therapist.

Last year, feeling at an all-time low, I decided it was time to start healing my wounded heart. I chose someone randomly, but luck was on my side. As soon as I stepped into Julia's neutral yet welcoming office, I knew I had made the right decision. I was a nervous wreck, but she promptly made me feel at ease with a voice as warm as honey. Soon, I was able to open up.

Week after week she has become my port in storm and I now wait with bated breath for each of our sessions. I'm so drawn to her. I'm convinced she's the soulmate I've always been searching for.

So, next time we meet, I will bite the bullet and pour my heart out. Love could be just around the corner.

~

## Céline Samson's Biography

Originally from France, Céline has now been living in London for 27 years where she works as an artist and translator/proofreader. In 2015 she published a book called *Three Seasons* combining texts and artworks.

www.celinesamson.co.uk/writings

## 55: HOODWINKED

*by Mangal Patel*

"Down in the dumps? You should be over the moon, married to Maid Marion."

"Yea, but my cupboard's bare and she's so high maintenance."

"C'mon, lighten the load. Tell me what's really on your mind." Little John remains cool as a cucumber.

"I'm sick as a parrot. Between a rock and a hard place. It used to be easy as pie, stealing from the rich to give to the poor."

"How about taxing the rich to give to the poor?"

"The Barons won't stand for it. Marion will dump me. She's not cut out for living below the poverty line."

"Let's turn this on its head. Tax the poor to give to the rich. A penny tax on the masses will raise more. Besides, beggars can't be choosers."

As the penny dropped, Robin Hood winked. In pulling the hood over impoverished eyes, he coined the phrase Hoodwinked.

~

## Mangal Patel's Biography

Mangal, a recent entrant to the wonderful world of writing, has a number of short stories published on the web and in hardback anthologies. She is a retired IT Director, is married and has twins. Lives in London, UK.

# 56: WATCHING YOU – WATCHING ME – WATCHING YOU

## *by David Turnbull*

"This is the scene where you are watching a film which shows you watching a film which shows you getting killed while you are watching a film which shows you getting killed," said the director.

"And I get killed while watching it?" asked the actor.

The director nodded.

"It's the defining moment of film. Life imitating art imitating life."

"What's my motivation?" asked the actor.

"Make your imitation of life imitating art as lifelike and artistic as possible."

On the set the film played out. At the point when the actor was watching himself get whacked on the head with a cricket bat while watching himself get whacked on the head with a cricket bat he was whacked on the head with a cricket bat.

Blood splattered the lens.

"That was a load of rubbish," said yet another version of the actor.

And was promptly whacked on the head...

~

# David Turnbull's Biography

David Turnbull is a Scotsman who live in London. He is a member of the Clockhouse London group of genre writers. Most recently *Ghost Highways* Midnight Street Press and *Forever Vacancy* Colours in Darkness.

www.tumsh.co.uk

# 57: BEST SERVED COLD

## *by Maddy Hamley*

The dark and stormy night rumbled through the mouldy, dank dungeon.

"Dressed to kill, I see." The man smirked and sipped his wine, red as blood.

The third princess shrugged. "Just going out on a limb. You seem like a guy who could do with a blushing bride."

"Not for lack of trying," he purred. "My wives keep getting into accidents."

The princess rolled her eyes. "My sister would get into... accidents. Did Rosella smell a rat when you gave her the wine?"

"So young and foolish," the man sighed theatrically.

The princess frowned. "And when Boudica came to save her?"

"Single combat."

The princess tutted. "Always playing the hero."

"Not unlike yourself," the man added. He raised his glass.

"Ah," she said. "But I'm a loose cannon."

Quick as a flash, she drew her pistol. A shot echoed in the dark.

~

## Maddy Hamley's Biography

Maddy Hamley is a bilingual English-German translator and full-time project manager. When she's not busy cursing at untranslatable Bavarian proverbs, she enjoys writing short stories, singing, or lounging around in Cologne with her fiancée.
   www.madham.org

## 58: NEW BEGINNINGS

### *by Jack Hanlon*

Greetings, on this dark and stormy night. We hope you share our excitement for this exclusive peek at our product. A word to the wise: Security are armed to the teeth.

Critics say we've put our eggs in one basket, but they're golden. Those who purchase this gadget will be the cats who got the cream.

First things first, introducing the inventor. Formerly a loose cannon, burning the candle at both ends, his exploits filled the tabloids. Airing your dirty washing in public is never ideal, but it was all fun and games. Against all odds, given a clean slate, he's transformed. All's well that ends well.

Despite no expense being spared during appliance construction, he's adopted an effective attitude, working his fingers to the bone, assembling this ace up his sleeve.

Without further ado, presenting the record breaking, risk taking son of his Mum. Put your hands together for...

~

## Jack Hanlon's Biography

All my life I've been telling tales and making up stories. I enjoy reading a diverse mix of genres and incorporating as many as I can into my writing. My favourite genre would probably be contemporary fantasy.

## 59: THE BRAVE STAY DRY

### *by David Silver*

The rain is coming down in stair rods as I wend my way along the streets of this concrete jungle I call home. It's a tough city, but it's my city.

Suddenly, I am hailed from a store doorway. "Remember me, Sarge?"

I have nerves of steel but, to tell you the truth, my blood freezes.

I peer into the darkness and, the next thing I know, a flash of lightning reveals the man's face.

"You," I gasp, a shiver running down my spine. I have seen a ghost.

"Yes, it's me, Kowalski, the battle-hardened vet who wiped out that machine-gun nest single-handed before throwing himself onto the grenade to save the new guy in the squad. War is hell, but I survived."

Kowalski sticks out a hand to check if it is still raining cats and dogs. "Doorways, huh? Still, any port in a storm."

~

## David Silver's Biography

David Silver was a reporter, sub-editor and columnist on various newspapers in Greater Manchester, England. He retired in 2002 and from 2011-2016 wrote a column for *The Courier*, a weekly newspaper for UK expatriates in Spain.

## 60: THE HAUNTING

### *by Julie Webb*

A cheeky-faced boy in shorts and a flat cap stared at the toy clown. It sat on a rocking chair which creaked as the doll's painted face came to life. "Who do we have here then?" it said.

"Eyup, my name is Sid," the boy said, in a bread-advert accent. "Have you seen my friend, Rebecca? She's pretty, wearing a floaty nightgown and crying over girl's things."

"Oh yes, we met. Mawhahaha, she…" The clown paused. "Wait, are you the seventh son of a seventh son? And is that scruffy dog yours?" Lucky the dog grabbed the clown. "Let me go you brute." Lucky obliged and the doll flew into the fire. "Noooo…" he called, as he sizzled out of existence.

Slowly, a cupboard door swung open and there stood Rebecca. "Who do we have here then?" she said.

~

## Julie Webb's Biography

Julie Webb is a biology lecturer and science communicator in Cambridge UK. Sometimes she experiments with fiction writing.

# 61: BASEBALL

## *by Ron Hall*

The catcher was quick as a cat and pounced on the ball.

The runner went lickety-split.

The ball travelled on a line to second.

The runner was as fast as lightning and he was safe.

The shortstop flopped like a fish and yelled, "Get the ball."

The runner sprang up like gas prices and headed for third. He didn't know the coach was as sneaky as a snake and the pitcher had the ball.

The runner was out at third before he even knew what happened and he was as mad as an old wet hen.

~

## Ron Hall's Biography

Ron Hall obtained his MBA from Letourneau University in Longview, Texas. He is the author of two Christian Fiction novels. Currently, Ron lives in Arkansas with his wife and five children.

## 62: KEEPING HIS COOL

### by Frank Hubeny

Robert Roketscienski's luck was running out. His students accused him of trying to dump their consciousness into an innocent computer. He told them they didn't have any consciousness to dump. That's why nothing happened, but he'd follow his star wherever its dark matter leads.

The universe, however, had other plans. Patricia Payninbut, Head of the Decoherence Department, waltzed into his office dressed to kill in high heels, miniskirt and enhanced body parts twinkling her baby blues.

"Don't sit there."

She sat there and Robert lost it. He jumped at her and she giggled. She only started screaming when she realised he was dragging her outside and bolting the door.

Now what? Should he tell Patricia the truth, that a wormhole in a parallel universe collapsed its wave function when she sat on it? Who would believe something like that? No. He'd keep his cool. Nature loves to run its course.

~

# Frank Hubeny's Biography

Frank Hubeny lives near Chicago and participates in two writers' groups, the Illinois State Poetry Society and the Prairie Writers Guild. He contributes prompts to dVerse Poets Pub.

www.frankhubeny.blog

## 63: EVERY CLOUD...

### *by Gavin Biddlecombe*

*Where'd he go?* she thought, finishing tying her skates. He'd vanished into thin air. Jane made her way to the ice rink.

"What're you doing down there?" she laughed, looking over the wall.

"I'm barking up the wrong tree," he replied. He paused as she stepped onto the ice, sliding across gracefully. "Whereas you take to it like a duck to water."

"You were chomping at the bit," she said, skating over.

"I believe," he smiled, "you can't teach an old dog new tricks." Before having the chance to stabilise himself, his legs shot out from under him. Trying desperately to grab him, Jane lost her footing, ending up flat on the ice beside him.

"It goes without saying," he groaned, "this is very painful."

"If you think about it, every cloud has a silver lining."

"Why do you say that?"

"We've already got ice for our bumps and bruises."

~

## Gavin Biddlecombe's Biography

Gavin lives in Gibraltar with his wife and crazy little dog where he spends his free time reading, writing short stories and working on his photography. His focus at the moment is on short stories and flash fiction.
www.gavinbiddlecombe.wordpress.com

## 64: THE WRITING ON THE WALL

*by Neil Brooks*

The rat ran up the drainpipe and was gone in the blink of an eye. It would turn up again like a bad penny, it was just a matter of time. The writing was on the wall for this old bag of bones. I used to be as fit as a fiddle, but my rat catching days were numbered and I felt as useful as a chocolate teapot.

Although weak as a kitten, I still had all my faculties and was as sharp as a tack – there are no bats in my belfry. I always say, "If life gives you lemons, then make lemonade." The day has not yet dawned for me to hang up my cap, so I soldier on one day at a time, putting one foot in front of the other and never counting my chickens. I still had a trick or two up my sleeve.

~

## Neil Brooks' Biography

Aged 56, living in North East Scotland. Hobbies are hillwalking, woodworking, DIY and drinking real ale. I like malt whisky. I have done a variety of jobs from engineer, masseur, lecturer, landscape gardener and customer advisor. I'm a writer now.

# 65: MY MATE NEXT DOOR

## *by Betty Hattersley*

My mate's family are a bit strange. It's all kipper and curtains in their house. His mum's always done up like a dog's dinner, dashing about like a blue arsed fly.

His dad's as thick as a plank, a right daft ha'p'orth. He's been on the treacle stick for years, but gets as drunk as a bobowler most nights.

My mate's alright though, he just has a lick and a promise, then runs like the clappers out of his house, before his old man gives him a fourpenny one. Any road up got to go tar-rah-for-a bit.

~

## Betty Hattersley's Biography

I've been writing for many years and have had numerous poems and short stories published in anthologies, newspapers, calendars and magazines.

I've written a small book (yet to be published) about the funny side of my outside catering days.

# 66: RHYME OR REASON

## *by Richard Swaine*

Combing my mane, I checked for perhaps the millionth time that my share of the carved-up spoils befitted a jungle beast of my stature, before wracking my brain – hey, any breadcrumb trail would do – as to how in heaven and earth I now found myself in this larger-than-life envelope, a papery shroud that every so often bulged on one side as something from without gave it a hefty nudge, an action regular as clockwork. Such a shame when, hitherto, my thoughts had been so taken up with the cobalt expanse above.

Clearly caught on the horns of a less-than-everyday occurrence, I hitched up the hosiery I'd recently taken to wearing and peered, owl-like, over the edge of this, my hopefully temporary accommodation. Further shock and awe ensued as I surmised I'd risen to the top of a tall, thin, positively flagpole-like structure. Of course, I'd little choice but to bite.

~

# Richard Swaine's Biography

In common with many budding writers, married father of one Richard's lifelong dream is to one day walk into a bookshop and find his title there on the shelves – whether it would actually sell any copies is the part he doesn't dwell on too much.

## 67: RELATIONSHIP WOES

### *by Jack Caldwell-Nichols*

*For goodness sake, Dave, I'm at my wits end. You're all talk and no action*, thought Jennifer calmly, as they enjoyed a stroll along the beach. Dave had been talking about buying her a diamond ring, something different to make her stand out from the crowd. A huge crowd.

*When is he going to just bite the bullet and propose?* her mind wandered tranquilly.

"I love you, Dave, so much. You are my everything. I couldn't possibly live without you," said she, wistfully.

\*

Dave didn't hear. He was going to throw in the towel. This was it. The calm before the storm. He had been trying to put it out of sight, so that it was out of mind, but it was an uphill battle. It was the moment of truth.

"Jennifer, I can't do it, it's over."

He then proceeded to jump in the sea and swim to France.

~

## Jack Caldwell-Nichols' Biography

Hailing from the hills, high in the north beyond Hadrian's Wall comes myself, Jack Caldwell-Nichols. A lover of the craft, taking inspiration from classic British comedy such as *Red Dwarf* to Stephen King's novels. I'll leave you to judge...

## 68: ALL'S WELL THAT ENDS WELL

### by Margaret Stokes

The new chemistry teacher was a pain in the neck. She had eyes in the back of her head. If someone only whispered, her eagle eye searched them out. She was a far cry from their previous master who was one of the lads.

After a lesson of blood sweat and tears, she got on her high horse with the head honcho of 5A and drove him up the wall.

On Tuesday she was at a conference so, boys being boys, a group lifted her little Fiat over a wall into the school rockery. Opportunity doesn't knock twice, so they seized the day and deposited it between a rock and a hard place. It was easier said than done.

She eventually returned. The moment of truth. Nobody let the cat out of the bag.

"OK, if it gets put back, I will forgive and forget."

~

## Margaret Stokes's Biography

Margaret Stokes is an old gal who loves playing with words and has found a great outlet for her obsession, a bit like her discovery of belly dancing after a lifetime of trying to ignore her hips.

## 69: IT TAKES TWO TO TANGO

### *by Sue Partridge*

Their eyes met across the crowded room. As the band struck up 'It's Now or Never', Jimmy swept across the dance floor.

"Fancy meeting you here. Shall we dance?"

"To be honest with you, I've got two left feet," replied Edna.

"Don't worry, it's as easy as one two three, let's give it a whirl."

They set off at a cracking pace.

"Hold your horses," cried Edna, "I'll never be the belle of the ball."

"You can say that again," agreed Jimmy. "I think we're flogging a dead horse here, let's cut our losses and throw in the towel."

"Yes, you can't teach an old dog new tricks," Edna laughed. "It's time I made tracks."

"Can I walk you home, Edna? Your place or mine?"

"You're a smooth operator, Jimmy. In your dreams."

Jimmy sloped off, his tail between his legs. "Ah well, there are plenty more fish in the sea."

~

## Sue Partridge's Biography

Sue Partridge is a retired finance officer who has recently discovered the fun of writing short stories and flash fiction. She is a member of a supportive writing group which offers the opportunity to experiment with new ideas.

## 70: OPPOSITES ATTRACT

*by Arlene Everingham*

She was a big-busted blonde, with one thing on her mind.

He was a beer-bellied, corn-fed hick with one foot in the grave.

When their eyes met across a crowded room, they both knew they were onto something.

Assuming he had a snowball's chance in hell, he decided that nothing ventured, nothing gained, so he sidled up to her at the bar. He looked her over, and she was armed to the teeth with beauty. He had butterflies in his stomach because he'd been hit with an ugly stick, but he was dressed to the nines.

"I'm going out on a limb here, but can I buy you a drink?" he asked. "I've got money to burn."

At first, cool as a cucumber, she lit up like a Christmas tree at these words.

It was a piece of cake from there, but only time will tell.

~

## Arlene Everingham's Biography

Arlene Everingham does archery and writes for fun. She lives in Luxembourg with her husband, four cats, an overflowing library, and an unruly garden.

## 71: JIM

### *by Bridget Scrannage*

"Old Jim's propping up the bar again, drunk as a skunk."

"Aye, three sheets to the wind."

"He's a chip off the old block."

"His father was a loose cannon when he'd had a few."

"Used to air his dirty laundry."

"Opened up many cans of worms."

"Always telling cock and bull stories."

"Jumped to conclusions."

"Regularly upset the apple cart."

"Jim's under his wife's thumb though."

"She's hard as nails."

"Screams at him like a fish wife."

"A force to be reckoned with."

"Remember when she caught him with his pants down, naked as a jaybird?"

"He bit off more than he could chew, seducing that barmaid."

"The old bag hauled him over the coals for that. If looks could kill."

"He's permanently in the doghouse now."

"Drove him to drink."

"Poor Jim."

"Aye, poor old Jim."

"Another beer, mate?"

"Wouldn't look a gift horse in the mouth."

~

## Bridget Scrannage's Biography

Bridget Scrannage lives near Bath with her husband and two deranged guinea pigs. She's been a self-employed secretary for 25 years. Bridget enjoys writing comedy, and is the founder of a writers' community with more than 100 members worldwide.

www.bridgetscrannage.wordpress.com/

# 72: FISH OUT OF WATER

## *by David Wright*

"Three hours and not a sausage, we're flogging a dead horse here."

"Beggars can't be choosers, it's the only spot left. Let's bide our time."

"You're the boss. Nothing ventured nothing gained."

"There's plenty of fish in the sea, or river, in our case."

"I'm on pins and needles waiting for the first catch."

"My line's taught, this is the moment of truth, keep your fingers crossed."

"Hope it's not a red herring – ha ha."

"Here it comes, the moment of truth."

"Keep your fingers crossed."

"Bother, I've lost it. I thought it was cut and dry."

"Ah well, back to the drawing board, no point in crying over spilt milk."

"I'm determined to catch one by hook or by crook."

"Let's call a spade a spade and go home and get some beers, we can start with a clean slate tomorrow."

~

## David Wright's Biography

I enjoy writing, playing the guitar for pleasure and volunteering at a local folk museum.

## 73: ALLEN'S WEDDING

### *by Prajith Menon*

"Early to bed, early to rise. I just can't wait for tomorrow.

"Tomorrow my brother is getting hitched. Allen knocked up Susan and now they are going to have a shotgun wedding. I wouldn't look for a shotgun wedding, I would look for a number that can settle the situation. I thought he was a geek but turned out to be a diamond in the rough.

"He's the big cheese at Intel Corporation. Even I tried to make it through but I realised I was just spinning my wheels.

"No family is perfect. I fight with him, but if anyone lays a finger on him, it makes my blood boil.

"I was the last person to enter the wedding hall. I got in under the wire. My parents read me the riot act for coming late. I wished him, 'Happy married life, take a chill pill.'"

~

## Prajith Menon's Biography

Prajith Menon was born in India. He lives in the United Arab Emirates. When people ask, "Did you always want to be a writer?" he says, "No – I have always been a writer." *Game for Game* was his debut novel.
www.linkedin.com/in/prajith-menon-694079132/

## 74: BRASSED OFF

*by Alicia Sledge*

Full of himself, Douglas knocked on Fred's door.

"I've a bone to pick with you. I'm at the end of my tether. Your blasted trumpet is the last straw, the straw that breaks the camel's back. I'm sick and tired of my evenings being disturbed. I'm not going to beat about the bush any longer. I've come to give it to you straight. Your racket is loud enough to wake the dead."

"Keep your hair on. That's like the pot calling the kettle black," Fred replied. "I think you're making a mountain out of a molehill. Anyway, your mowing the grass before 8am is enough to try the patience of a saint."

Douglas looked crestfallen. Suddenly Fred's voice was nice as pie and he held out his hand. "Why don't we bury the hatchet? At the end of the day, we don't want any bad blood. Let bygones be bygones?"

~

## Alicia Sledge's Biography

Alicia enjoys writing stories and poems, some of which you will find on her blog. She also reads avidly, paints, and makes 1/12th scale dolls house miniatures. She's recently had a story shortlisted and published by Stringybark Stories in Australia.

www.sledgendswriting.blogspot.co.uk

## 75: A PIZZA THE ACTION

*by Franca Basta*

She sipped her cocktail as the Italian stallion propped up the bar. Their eyes met and he was over like a shot.

"Do you come here often?" he asked.

She fluttered her eyelashes, at a loss for words.

"I want us to make sweet music together," he said.

'Nessun Dorma' played in the background.

"Is that Coldplay?" she enthused, thick as two short planks.

"Mamma mia," he gesticulated wildly, but decided to let it drop. "Let's go to my mother's for a bite to eat. Her spaghetti is to die for."

She knew Italian mothers ruled the roost, but had to come clean, spill the beans and put her cards on the table. "Pasta's not my cup of tea."

Stunned silence. The dye was cast, the chips were down, it was over before it had begun.

"This is arrivederci," he announced coldly.

"Really? But I ordered a piña colada."

~

## Franca Basta's Biography

Franca Basta is a bi-lingual English language teacher and proud grandmother. She belongs to an international creative writing group and has had articles published in the Italian magazine *Giovani Genitori*. She lives in Italy with her husband of 40 years.

## 76: TOUCHING BASE

### by Kathryn Evans

"So, Nigel, I need you to hit the ground running. This new logo you're designing has got to be something really iconic."

"OK, Dave, you can count on me to give 150%. We're definitely singing from the same hymn sheet."

Dave's my boss. He's a real high flier at the top of his game. I'm more of a team player, but sometimes feel like I go under the radar.

"You've hit the nail on the head there, Nigel. With some joined up thinking, the sky's the limit. Failure is not an option."

"That's a bit of a well-worn cliché, Dave, if you don't mind me saying."

"Oh... Anyway, going forward, we agree that you'll ping me the new logo by close of play tomorrow."

"Yes, Dave. At the end of the day, I believe that the customer is always right, so I'll do whatever it takes."

~

## Kathryn Evans' Biography

Kathryn Evans was born in Wales, raised in Scotland, has an Irish grandfather and lives in Plymouth, England. She studied genetics to PhD level. Her main passion is rock/indie music.

## 77: CHARLIE & DEIDRE

*by Malcolm Richardson*

Charlie was a big cheese in the city. Deidre, his wife, was just cheesed off.

Every day he woke at the crack of dawn, up like a lark and off like a bat out of hell. Late nights at the office meant Deidre stayed home twiddling her thumbs, lying in bed counting sheep.

One day, she decided enough was enough, she was going to paint the town red and spice up her life. She'd heard there was a new kid on the block. He was the bee's knees and she wanted a taste of his honey.

They met one night at the dark end of the street. He swept her off her feet and they danced the night away.

Charlie crawled in after midnight to an empty bed and a note.

"The bird in the hand has flown, spread my wings and taken flight. See you later alligator."

~

## Malcolm Richardson's Biography

Malcolm first wrote about cycle races for magazine articles. He progressed to writing fiction; with numerous short stories in his bottom drawer, he is approaching completion of a novel first draft. Recently, he discovered flash fiction. Malcolm resides in Warwickshire.

www.lieshalftruthsfiction.wordpress.com

# 78: THE PEP TALK

## *by Angela P Googh*

The usual summary of how well we are doing...

"But we don't want to kill the goose that laid the golden egg. We need to go the extra mile. We have got to keep our shoulders to the wheel and our noses to the grindstone.

"Let me deal with the politics. I do not mind taking one for the team.

"'Plunk down, get your head in the game and keep your eye on the prize. I know you all want to give 110%."

Applause.

"Thank you. Really, I'm glad to be here for the team."

After...

"Why do I always come out of those meetings dog tired?"

"Perhaps you have a bone to pick?"

"What? And see the man about a dog. That would put me in the hot seat."

"There is no I in team."

"'No. It is what it is. I'll just have to grin and bear it."

~

## Angela P Googh's Biography

Angela P Googh is a computer programmer, predominantly with information database systems. She is married with two grown children, active in her church, an amateur genealogist, and green, except for her thumbs. Angela lives in Waterloo, Ontario, Canada.

Find Angela on Twitter: @angelagoogh

# 79: THE OPEN AIR CONCERT

## *by Wendy Kelly*

A dull roar erupted from the groupies when the leading lady rocked onto the stage. She was the size of a double-decker bus and done up like a Christmas tree. The night was promising to be a blast, (in more ways than one) as the heavens opened and rain bucketed down.

"Good weather for ducks," she bellowed, "but the show must go on."

With a voice like a foghorn, she belted out her opening number. It went from bad to worse. She was so off her game tonight. The audience booed and hissed as the band played on. It was indeed all over when the fat lady sang.

~

## Wendy Kelly's Biography

No author biography supplied.

# 80: A WINTER'S TALE

## *by Abigail Rowe*

"Not a ghost of a chance," she sighed. In the dead of winter, earth hard as iron, her footsteps echoed in the still air, as, cold as ice, she trod her weary way towards the warm glow of home, sweet home.

In times gone by, they had beaten a path to her door, a happy throng. Now there was one solitary traveller, and she couldn't expect him to brave the elements. She'd have to face it on her own.

But hark, the distant hum of a motor.

"Fat chance," muttered the devil on one shoulder.

"Keep the faith," cried the angel on the other.

As plain as day, she saw bright lights in the distance and dared to dream.

\*

"Happy Christmas, Mum." His voice rang out clear as a bell.

"Oh Mikey, I'd lost all hope in you getting here."

"Miss your festive cheer? Not a snowball's chance in hell."

~

## Abigail Rowe's Biography

Abigail Rowe lives in Cork, Ireland. She has rather too much fun writing flash fiction and poetry whilst working on her first novel. Her publishing debut of two pieces may be found in the *Grindstone Anthology 2017*.

Find Abigail on Twitter: @RoweWrites

# 81: SEEK ME

## *by Sara Siddiqui Chansarkar*

Someone's Tinder profile:

All the world's a stage.

When I play the waiter, too many cooks spoil the broth and I end up with peanuts in my pockets. I see red and throw in my towel.

When I play the carpenter, everyone has an axe to grind with me. I lay down my tools to bury the hatchet.

But the ship never sinks for a man for all seasons. Another day, another dollar.

To a jaded eye, mine would look like a face only a mother could love, but you know that appearances are deceptive.

All said and done, I am a diamond in the rough waiting for you to polish me. Together we can be happy as larks.

But don't sit stewing around, for – though I hate tooting my horn – the likes of me sell like hotcakes.

I don't want you crying your eyes out over spilled milk.

~

## Sara Siddiqui Chansarkar's Biography

Sara is an Indian American. She was born in a middle-class family in India. Her poems, stories and essays have appeared in print and online. She is a Pushcart nominee for 2017. She can be reached on Twitter @PunyFingers.

www.saraspunyfingers.com

## 82: GUMSHOE

### *by Bryan Keefe*

I wake to sunlight filtering through the blinds and a ringing in my ears. I'd gone to sleep cuddling the phone again. I uncurled from the office couch and empty bottles fell to the floor. One hell of a night.

"Dick Rake," I slurred, answering the phone.

It was a doll and she had a case. She'd be down in five.

She walked in and she was something else. She looked as though she had been poured into her dress but the dress was a pint pot and she was definitely a quart.

Her old man was missing. Not much of a case, but I took it. I needed the dough. Time to hit the streets and follow leads, but my dog walking business could wait. I had a case to solve and I needed a drink. I was thinking Kale with a touch of Lemongrass.

Dick Rake was back.

~

## Bryan Keefe's Biography

I am a 60 year old retired policeman from Essex. Nowadays, I fill my time with cycling and keeping fit.

## 83: NO PAIN, NO GAIN

*by Dee La Vardera*

Yes, it's been rejected again. My agent says, "Derivative, unoriginal and clichéd. Have you thought of taking up painting?"

How dare she? This is my raison d'être, my way of life, my bread and butter. The reason I get up in the morning. I've worked my socks off to finish my magnum opus. Clichéd? Poppycock. Give up writing? I should cocoa.

I have so much more to give. That novel was just the tip of the iceberg. I'm champing at the bit with the next big idea. Got an ace opening: 'It is a truth universally acknowledged, that a single man...'

Another agent? No way, José. Avoid them like the plague. I'll go it alone. Only time will tell, but I feel it in my waters – I will survive.

I'm a glass half full kinda gal. I'll be top of the bestsellers list this time next year.

~

## Dee La Vardera's Biography

Dee La Vardera, writer and photographer, born a Brummie, now a Moonraker, lives a short distance from Silbury Hill and Avebury Stone Circle. 'If you can't find inspiration round here, then you must be dead from the neck up.'

www.dewfall-hawk.com

## 84: JUNGLE TRAVEL

*by Ron Smith*

It's as hot as hell and I am sweating like a pig. My armpits must smell like a Turkish wrestler's jockstrap. I feel like I could eat a horse, but I'd prefer to be cool as a cucumber and as fresh as a daisy.

The leeches are clinging on like leeches. There are snakes in the grass, alligators in the rivers crying crocodile tears and piranha waiting to strip the flesh off our bones. A fine kettle of fish, as you might say.

We are between a rock and a hard place and doing our best to travel as the crow flies.

Against all odds, we burst into the sunlight and make tracks, full steam ahead to the guest house.

Today we have managed to go the extra mile and we are on cloud nine. I intend to get as drunk as a handcart (as they say in Somerset).

~

## Ron Smith's Biography

Ron Smith is a retired engineer, aviation enthusiast and historian. He has written around a dozen aviation-related books and is branching out into light-hearted fiction and creative writing.

www.ronandjimsmith.com

# 85: ROMANCE NEVER DIES

## *by Aleksandra Petrovic*

"Dearly beloved…"

Those words sent chills down Stacy's spine. The instinct to tear the train off her dress and bail was stilled by Rick's dominant grip on her hand. It shouldn't – couldn't – end like this, marrying this brute whom her family misguidedly idolised.

But Danny, the sweet nerdy boy she loved, had disappeared. Months of silence and Rick's insistence had led her to duly accept his proposal and resign herself to this fate.

Just before she was about to choke out the, "I do," a rumble sounded from outside, coming rapidly closer until the chapel doors burst open and an onyx motorcycle charged up the aisle to the shocked cries of the wedding guests and stopped short in front of the couple.

The motorcyclist pulled off his helmet and ran a hand through his hair.

"Danny," cried Stacy, dropping the bouquet and flinging herself into his arms.

~

VOLUME 1

# Aleksandra Petrovic's Biography

Aleksandra Petrovic was born in Serbia and raised on the sunny island of Cyprus. Obtaining her Bachelor's and Master's degrees in London, she has since worked in a number of countries in Europe and is currently residing in Barcelona.

## 86: JUST A MATTER OF TIME

### *by Gary McGrath*

The stereotype clichéd, as the printed words formed on the casting plate.

"Mon Dieu," said Pierre, as his beret tipped over his eyes and his string of onions round his neck almost got caught in the press.

"Don't get your knickers in a twist," said Harold, his English assistant. "You'll never get back on your bike with twisted knickers, my old china."

"Mais oui," said Pierre. "But read between the lines. This writing is a code."

"Blimey," said Harold. "You could be right. Only time will tell, but you may have discovered this in the nick of time."

"I think my countrymen are preparing to surrender," cried Pierre.

"Well," said Harold. "It was just a matter of time…"

~

## Gary McGrath's Biography

Currently writing an autobiography entitled *The Man Without a Plan*.

I enjoy being playful where possible.
I believe life is for living. Fun is important.
I mean nobody any harm and I come in peace.
Take me to your reader.
Find Gary on Twitter: @TheOtherVoice

## 87: RUDE AWAKENING, FRONT ROW, ADVANCED WRITING CLASS IN ENGLISH AS A SECOND LANGUAGE

*by Amanda Garzia*

I have a bone to pick with Mr Ford. I deserved an A+. Gabriella, that thick-headed blonde, most certainly did not.

But why jump to conclusions so hastily? Per carità, I haven't even seen my paper yet. Maybe he doesn't have it in for me after all. Maybe I'll wait before screaming blue murder.

Chin up. Fingers crossed. That's the spirit. It's only a matter of time before he figures out there's been a mistake. The next thing I know he'll be bending over backwards to apologize. It cannot be otherwise: my grasp of the language is second to none. Just listen to me, for heaven's sake, thinking this through in flawless English.

There he comes, essays in hand.

"Some of you – unwittingly, of course – went overboard with hackneyed phrases, making reading a tad mind-numbing. So today we'll be discussing clichés and how to avoid them like the plague."

~

## Amanda Garzia's Biography

At age 12, Amanda typed the first edition of her own (now defunct) magazine, posting copies to Canadian friends left behind on coming to Malta. Having written for *The Times of Malta*, *Pink*, and *Child*, she's presently concentrating on fiction.

www.facebook.com/mandy.garzia

## 88: A NEW BROOM

### *by Sue Johnson*

I was nervous as a cat on a hot tin roof about my new job. I was at the end of my tether with Rod, sick of him saying, "Pull yourself together. Nothing will come of it. It's only a cleaning job. You'll be back to square one in the blink of an eye."

All I wanted was a fighting chance – and to let my hair down without being constantly reminded that money doesn't grow on trees. Rod sounded like a broken record. Maybe it was time to bite the bullet and show him the door.

~

## Sue Johnson's Biography

Sue Johnson is a poet, short story writer and novelist. Her work is inspired by the countryside, eavesdropping in cafes and reading fairy-tales. Sue is a *Writing Magazine* Creative Writing Tutor and runs her own brand of workshops.

www.writers-toolkit.co.uk

## 89: DREAM HOME

*by Melanie Goodell*

Summer smiled coyly at Adam. "My dear, you're seeing this glass as half empty. This would be our dream come true."

Adam glanced back at her, annoyance clear in his expression. "Summer, not all that glitters is gold."

Summer felt as though her back were against the wall. "This is a golden opportunity. We should seize the day and jump on this bandwagon before it leaves the station."

Summer was, of course, referring to the house they were touring, sure they should buy the property. She could tell that Adam felt they were buying a pig in a poke, a money pit, a lost cause that would suck up all their money.

"Take a chance, darling. The possibilities are endless." She spun, arms wide.

"You've twisted my arm," he responded, finally smiling back at her enthusiasm.

They rushed back into the house to find the realtor, ready to grab life by the horns.

~

## Melanie Goodell's Biography

Melanie Goodell has been writing since she learned to spell. She recently finished her first adult novel and looks forward to the day she can write full time.

www.meligoodell.com

## 90: CARYS DUMBLEWAITE

### by Robbie Porter

Carys Dumblewaite was as old as the hills with a face like a well slapped bum. All she wanted to do was kiss and make up, but it had ended with her knickers in a twist. Literally.

She'd just got to grips with the mangle when he'd walked through the door to find her working the handle at the speed of light. Her smalls were on their way through.

"I'm rushed for time," she said. He pointed at her knickers, emerging from the mangle, and said, "What goes around comes around."

Well it's true what they say. Laughter is the best medicine. It was obvious he had his tail between his legs.

"I'm sorry," he said. "I woke up on the wrong side of the bed."

"There's no point crying over spilled milk," said Carys.

"All's well that ends well."

The good news is they both lived happily ever after.

~

## Robbie Porter's Biography

Robbie Porter is a lecturer and charity worker from Worcester, England. He has published two collections of 100 word stories, *The Dead Like To Dance Too...* and *The Ghosts and Ghouls Dating Agency*, both available on Amazon.

www.facebook.com/robbie.porter.37

## 91: NO MORE WORMS

### *by Claire Apps*

At the end of the day, what could she do? She was at her wit's end, nothing seemed to be going right. She was at the end of her rope. She had her back to the wall, it was now or never. No one else could help, they weren't in the same boat as her. She just couldn't beat around the bush anymore. She would have to go to her dad and ask for help. Well, beggars couldn't be choosers. At least it was better the devil you know than the devil you don't, she supposed.

She couldn't go and blow the whistle on her husband, it just wasn't right. The bottom line was she still loved him. The buck had to stop here, with her. No more opening cans of worms.

~

## Claire Apps' Biography

I have had some short stories and poems published. However, my main interest is teaching 'therapeutic creative writing'. I have run a therapeutic creative writing course for vulnerable women at the local Women's Centre for 3 years.

www.writing-experiment.com

# 92: THE DEVIL MAKES WORK FOR IDLE HANDS

*by Donna-Louise Bishop*

It was a dark and stormy night – which was to be expected after it had been raining cats and dogs all day long – when she realised her bundle of joy wasn't quite the ticket.

To complete strangers, the toddler looked as if butter wouldn't melt. To his mother, he was a force to be reckoned with. On a daily basis, he would scream from the rooftops, opening up a can of whoop-ass if demands weren't met, and fly off the handle at every little thing which wasn't up to scratch.

More than once she had wanted to abandon ship, to run away and join the circus, never to be seen again, but, deep down, she knew she loved the bones of him really.

He was the absolute spitting image of his father, and in more ways than one. After all, the acorn doesn't fall far from the tree.

~

## Donna-Louise Bishop's Biography

Donna-Louise Bishop is a regional journalist and creative writer from Norfolk, UK. Mum to three noisy boys, she enjoys writing micro fiction and is also editing her first novel. More of her experimental work can be found on her blog:

www.newshoundnovelist.wordpress.com

## 93: BEARING UP

*by Alan Pattison*

The project management meeting was a disaster.

I kicked off with the guy managing the timeline who said, "Sorry mate, but we're moving at a snail's pace and I don't know why."

"I don't want to chicken out, but I admit that the lion's share might be my team," said the IT expert. "Now, that has let the cat out of the bag."

"It seems to me," said one manager, "that there is an elephant in the room somewhere."

"Well, I intend to take a bird's eye view, make sure that we get all our ducks in a row and don't end up as a one trick pony."

"Or, even worse, end with a cock-up."

~

## Alan Pattison's Biography

I am a semi-retired former management consultant who researches and writes up local history along with writing poetry, fiction and possibly finishing my first novel.

# 94: DRESSED TO THE NINES

## *by Meg Gain*

Amy was all dressed up with nowhere to go.

"Always the bridesmaid, never the bride." The telephone rang. At the drop of a hat, her mood changed and, by the time Harry called, she felt like a new-born lamb skipping through a flowery meadow.

"Seems ages since I saw you," Harry said.

"But I waved like a flag the other evening in the Angel," Amy replied.

"I'm as useless as a lead balloon," Harry laughed like a drain.

"Where are we going?"

"As far as the eye can see," Harry joked.

Amy risked Harry's wrath. She was as meek as a lamb. It could be a nail in the coffin. They danced till the crack of dawn. Harry knew it was costing him an arm and a leg. Amy was worth it.

*Another day, another dollar*, Harry thought. *All bets are off as to where this romance will end.*

~

## Meg Gain's Biography

Jo from *Little Women* was my alter-ego as a child. I've been writing fiction and non-fiction since then. As a former librarian, I've spent my life surrounded by books by wonderful writers. They are a constant inspiration.

# 95: LET'S BEGIN WITH AN A

## *by Janet Lister*

At the last minute, my brother asked me to do him a favour. He expected me to agree to it at the drop of a hat. I normally have no axe to grind but really I was at my wits' end. I had to get up at the crack of dawn and then, armed to the teeth, find the field and shoot the pest.

As luck would have it, the beast appeared from nowhere, as plain as the nose on your face, but I was at a loss, at the end of my tether.

My brother is the apple of my eye and his farm is costing him an arm and a leg, but I am no assassin.

I thought, *As ye sow so shall ye reap*, and I couldn't do it. After all is said and done, at the end of the day, am I my brother's keeper?

~

## Janet Lister's Biography

Retired science teacher. Part of a writing group enjoying using Chris's site.

# 96: YOU COULD CUT IT WITH A KNIFE

## *by Ally Howie*

The Secretary of Defence chewed his half-finished cigar, oblivious to the tobacco juice running down his chin and staining his Marine Corp dress uniform.

"Mr President?" he urged, as he proffered the telephone receiver, its red helical cord stretching into a taut, quivering line.

The President stared blankly down the length of the mahogany table, seemingly oblivious to the tension in the room.

"Sir, Mr President, sir," the Secretary of Defence barked, his face becoming as red as the telephone he tendered, his voice as sharp as the stars on his lapel.

The leader of the western world nodded in resignation, placidly taking the telephone receiver with a resigned sigh.

"This is the President... Yeah... Pepperoni. Extra fries. Thanks."

The Secretary of Defence slumped into his chair as he slowly ran his hands through his buzz cut hair. "Pepperoni," he whispered to himself. "Every single week, it's pepper-freakin'-oni."

~

## Ally Howie's Biography

Ally is a perspiring writer (aspiring?, sorry, I'm not very good with words) living in Jersey – not New Jersey, the old one between Britain and French France.

# 97: ALL IN A DAY'S WORK

## *by Pat Hough*

Jack Tracey, ace detective, stared down at the corpse and looked at the blonde broad crying her eyes out.

"You're all dressed up and nowhere to go, baby. I'm all ears. Tell me, what happened? Come on, air your dirty laundry, why don't you?"

"I was frightened to death. The killer shot Harry and fled."

"You don't fool me. You married Harry for his dough. He didn't stand a chance. The writing on the wall says you killed your husband and the gun in your bag will prove it."

At the speed of light, Tracey overpowered the broad, wrestling the bag from her grasp.

Just then the police arrived.

"Reading between the lines, it looks as if you've solved the case again, Tracey."

"All in a day's work," Tracey replied. "I'm off to a bar. All work and no play make this Jack a dull boy."

~

# Pat Hough's Biography

Hi, my name is Pat Hough. I'm a dabbler in words, not a true 'wordsmith'. I enjoy writing and am always surprised when an initial idea turns itself into a plot with characters I become fond of.

## 98: THREE'S A CROWD

### *by Ann Tonge*

Ben was sleeping like a log when Dad stormed in and raised the alarm.

"Get up, lazy bones, she'll be home any minute now. Let's get this place as clean as a whistle."

His stepmother's bark may be worse than her bite, but it was better to be safe than sorry. He had a plan. A messy house would be like a red rag to a bull. Dad was rushing around frantically. Ben followed suit, like father like son, with a lick and a promise.

She flung open the door, then stopped in her tracks.

"Hats off to you, couldn't have done better myself. I'll take the hint. I'm needed round here like a fish needs a bicycle."

Ben sighed in relief. "Never mind, Dad, better to have loved and lost than never to have loved at all and, anyway, there's plenty more fish in the sea."

~

## Ann Tonge's Biography

Ann Tonge is a tutor and writer living in South Wales, who enjoys both academic and creative writing. When not with her six children and horde of grandchildren, or working on her novel, she can be found at:

www.ramblinganndotcom.wordpress.com

## 99: A MODERN LOVE STORY

### *by Rose Cheung*

Having just finished the play *Romeo and Juliet*, Ophelia was determined to love and be loved the way Juliet did.

She had thus found herself a Romeo. He was a popular student at her rival school, with features so handsome that he looked like an actual lord. Ophelia had never talked to the boy before, nor did she actually love him, but he bore the closest resemblance to the existence she was desperately trying to craft.

Never mind that he had a girlfriend. That girl would be Rosaline, someone so minor that Romeo would soon forget her, the moment he laid eyes on Juliet.

When Ophelia and the boy locked eyes for the very first time, she knew the tables were turning. He walked up to her and her heart pounded with excitement. What words of love would he speak?

"Stop following me, or I will call the police."

~

## Rose Cheung's Biography

Rose Cheung is from the vibrant city of Hong Kong. An English undergraduate student at the Chinese University, Rose spends her spare time writing, procrastinating and sleeping.

www.instagram.com/rosecheung/

## 100: THE WILL

### *by Molly Apps*

I was fit to be tied. We had fought like cats and dogs for over a year about that stupid will. He was filthy rich, he didn't need the money. It was all fine and dandy saying I was the second born but, for Pete's sake, saying I didn't deserve the money, well, that was the final straw.

I had told him to 'go jump in the lake', so to speak, and gone to the lawyers. I had told them how much he had gotten under my skin. They had replied, "Well, a good man is hard to find."

Today, after the hearing, he is green with envy. I had come out with my guns blazing. I didn't handle it with kid gloves. I went for the jugular. I'm as happy as a pig in mud. I won the case and got every penny. He… well… he lost everything.

~

## Molly Apps's Biography

I have only just started writing, with the help off my mother. This is my first attempt at a short story.

## A FINAL NOTE

Jude and I would like to say one last THANK YOU to all the authors featured in this anthology. Their generosity is helping support a very worthy charity and it's an honour to present their stories in this collection.

Don't forget to check my website for more writing challenges – there will be many more appearing in the future. You will be able to find all the details here: www.christopherfielden.com/writing-challenges/

I will say farewell Bristol-style:

Cheers me dears,

Chris Fielden

Printed in Great Britain
by Amazon